# RISKING IT ALL

*Hawk Brothers Romance # 4*

## CAMI CHECKETTS

*Birch River*
PUBLISHING

# COPYRIGHT

Edited by Daniel Coleman, Valerie Bybee, and Jenna Roundy.

# CHAPTER ONE

Avalyn Shaman exited her room at the beautiful Cancun resort and took the stairs six flights down. She couldn't wait to float in one of the infinity pools overlooking the beach. This five-star resort had so many pools she'd lost track. She'd arrived a day early for Creed Hawk and Kiera Richins's wedding. The three of them had been friends since childhood.

She adored the entire Hawk family, with the exception of the youngest brother, Bridger. He was a cocky extreme athlete who thought the women of the world were created to decorate his muscular arms. Bridger was two years younger than her and lived to torment her—teasing her whenever he saw her, lodging himself in her brain the rest of the time. It aggravated her to no end that she had dreams about him on a regular basis, and even during the day she couldn't get his handsome face out of her mind.

*No, thank you, brain. Please choose again.*

She exited the elevator and walked along the covered path

toward the closest section of pools. A large man stepped in her path. Avalyn skidded to a halt to avoid running into him, then made the mistake of looking past the muscular body to the man's face. Tanned skin, dark hair, deep brown eyes, the perfectly trimmed facial hair, and a permanent smirk on those intriguing lips. Bridger Hawk. Her heart rate picked up without her permission.

His dark eyes lit up, sparkling at her. "Ava Baby!" He wrapped his lean arms around her and lifted her off the ground, squeezing her tight against his bare chest in one of his famous bear hugs. She'd had her share of these hugs since childhood, but she could never stop her body from reacting. Her body was trembling and warm all over. She was an accomplished, self-made woman. Why did she have to react like a teenager every time she saw this beautiful man?

"Bridger," she sort of moaned out. No! Oh, no. She couldn't reveal how much he affected her; he'd laugh himself to sleep at night. He was a world-renowned extreme athlete who took nothing seriously, and she was a world-renowned philanthropist, author, and speaker. They had nothing in common, and she needed to stay far away from him.

He set her on her feet but kept her tight in his embrace. Avalyn's hands went to his chest to steady herself. Big mistake. The smooth skin and hard muscle there made her stomach fill with heat and desire that she had to squelch … and quick. She'd allowed him to kiss her once in high school. The beautiful connection had messed with her mind for years, especially since he'd kissed Kelly Turner the next day at lunch in front of the entire school and broken Avalyn's heart. She couldn't go back to those immature and stupid longings. She was way past all of that, way past Bridger Hawk. She just needed her heart to catch up with her brain.

He stared down at her with that trademark smirk on his lips. "Ava. I hoped you'd be here."

"Why?" What was wrong with her? Why was she reduced to these one-word answers? She needed to demand he release her, and she needed to take her hands off his chest pronto. She felt like she was in a cloud with him staring at her like she was his prize for winning the international surf competition.

Bridger simply smiled, bowed his head, and claimed her lips with his. Avalyn's body shoved her logical mind to the side as those perfect lips she'd had dream after dream about worked their brain-deceiving magic on her. She stood on tiptoes and pressed herself tighter against him, her hands sliding up his chest and around his neck. She wanted him closer, she wanted him to never stop kissing her, she wanted him …

No! This was Bridger Hawk. Heartbreaker extraordinaire. The world expert on claiming hearts and then shattering them.

Avalyn yanked herself away from him. Bridger unfortunately didn't release his grip on her waist, and instead of his trademark smirk, he was pulling in quick breaths and staring at her like his mind was as cloudy as hers was.

"Avalyn," he murmured, his gaze full of wonder and desire. Then he pulled her in again, and heaven help her, she didn't put up an ounce of resistance. Truth be known, she urged him closer. His mouth was full and warm and his muscular frame surrounded her. She couldn't escape, and she didn't want to. The kiss took on a life of its own, and Avalyn had no choice but to surrender to the desire she'd always had to be in Bridger's arms, to kiss him, to know she was the only woman in the world for him.

No! She wasn't the one for him. She was one of thousands of women he kissed while thousands more waited for their chance to have the superstar give them one glance, smile, or touch.

She wrenched her mouth free and slapped him hard across the jaw.

Bridger's eyes widened and he finally released her. They were both breathing heavily as they stood in the shaded walkway and stared at each other.

"Hi, Ava Baby," he murmured as if they'd just run into each other. His eyes slid over her floral one-piece swimsuit that was underneath her lacy cover-up. "You look ... amazing."

"What are you doing?" she demanded, folding her arms across her chest. He acted like she hadn't even slapped him. Like they hadn't even kissed. Dang him! Didn't those kisses mean anything to him? She knew they didn't, and the pain deepened. "You don't just kiss someone hello like that."

"I've been dreaming of doing that for years." His smirk reappeared briefly, and then his eyes went soft and warm as they studied hers. "I just had no idea it would feel like that. Just like in high school ... only ..." His voice trailed off.

"Only what?" *Be strong. He's a player. He's not your type. He'll break your heart all over again. Oh, have mercy. Why does he have to look at me like that?*

Bridger took a step closer, his large form overshadowing her. She glanced up to meet his gaze so she wouldn't focus on his beautifully formed chest. "Your kiss is like heaven," he murmured. He reached up and cupped her cheek with his palm, leaning down like he was going to kiss her again.

Avalyn's heart was thumping so high and fast she could hardly breathe, let alone speak. She had to be strong, though, or she would regret it forever. Bridger Hawk was not the man for her, no way, no how. "Do you want me to slap you again?"

The smolder in his dark eyes made her knees gooey. "For sure, if it means I can kiss you first."

Avalyn planted her hands on his firm chest and pushed hard. "Stop with your games, Bridger. I'm not a teenager anymore, and I'm not your hoochie of the week."

Bridger straightened and released her face. His brow furrowed. "So you do remember kissing me before you left for college?"

Avalyn's face heated up again. That kiss had been almost as good as the ones he'd just given her, but the mature man in front of her was much more irresistible than the teenage tease had been. Her eyes narrowed and she planted her hands on her hips. "So why was this kiss like heaven and the other one wasn't?"

Bridger grinned like he'd just won the X Games. "They were both like heaven. It's just been so many years I'd forgotten how heavenly you are, love. Can you help me remember again?" He moved in for more. The nerve of this man!

Avalyn backed away until she ran into the building. "No." Still, between him saying her kiss was like heaven and her easily remembering how his kiss had lit her up from the inside out, she wanted to throw herself into his arms again. What was wrong with her? She was a strong, driven woman. The men she dated were hardworking, well-known philanthropists like her who took life seriously and lived to help others. Bridger was a playboy who cared about nothing but his next thrill.

"No?" He arched an eyebrow as he tracked her movements like a panther. When he had her cornered against the wall, he planted his hands on either side of her head and leaned closer and closer. His breath brushed her cheek, and Avalyn quivered.

Maybe just one more kiss, and then she'd tell him off and stay far away from him.

She glanced up at those well-formed lips and found herself arching up to meet him. "No!" she yelled, pushing at his bulging chest muscles yet again. "I am done kissing you, Bridger Hawk."

He blew out a breath and smiled. "Ah, well. You can't blame a guy for trying."

"That's what you think!" She ducked under his arm and then pivoted to face him.

He slowly straightened and smirked at her again. His beautiful body was on fine display in nothing but a gray swimsuit. She supposed he had to be in good shape to excel at so many different sports like he did. Not that she watched his YouTube channel fanatically or something. She watched a video here and there, but once a week was all she allowed herself. Okay, that was a lie. It was one a day, and she only allowed herself five minutes of viewing Bridger time, like savoring a piece of Ghirardelli chocolate after a hard day.

She held up a hand and shook her finger at him, which only made him smile even bigger." Now you listen here," she said. "You stay away from me the next two days. You don't kiss me, smile at me, or corner me in hallways."

Bridger arched his eyebrows. "So no more kissing and slapping? I can't even smile?" He tried for a serious expression, but it just didn't suit him.

"Stop playing stupid, Bridger. We both know how smart you are. Just because you squander yourself with women who only want you for your body and your fame doesn't mean you're an idiot."

His face only tightened for a beat; then he grinned and sidled closer to her. "Somewhere in that irritated speech, I think there was a compliment. You like my body and you think I'm brilliant?"

Avalyn pulled in a shaky breath. She had to get far away from this man and never, ever be alone with him. "Listen closely, Bridger Hawk. I've been nice to you because of my respect for your parents and brothers. I did not come here to see you, and I will *never* allow you to kiss me again."

His eyes grew serious, but his words were teasing as always. "You sure? You seemed to enjoy the kisses as much as I did. You know how I like to 'play stupid,' but I could've sworn you kissed me back, threw your arms around my neck, felt up my chest." He flexed his chest, making his pec muscles dance.

Avalyn's jaw dropped. He was out of control.

He tilted his head and gave her a significant look. "Was I daydreaming all of that?"

"Yes! Just because you're the stuff that every woman's daydreams are made of does not mean I like you or want you around, got it?" Shoot, she kept slipping words in there that would make him think she did like him.

He nodded, folding his arms across his chest, which made his biceps bulge. She was too strong to fall into petty physical attraction and womanly desires for Bridger Hawk. He had plenty of women chasing him at all times. He did not need her. She did not need him.

"You only want me for the conquest," she said.

His eyebrows rose again, but he didn't even attempt to dispute that.

"I am not your plaything, Bridger. I know we go way back, but all you've done your entire life is tick me off." *And make me want to kiss you.* The kisses had been so mind-blowing that she still couldn't screw her head on straight.

"I'm sorry, Ava Baby. I've never wanted to tick you off."

"Stop calling me Ava Baby," she ground out. "And you'll stay away from me if you know what's good for you."

She should tell him off some more, but she had to get away. If he gave her one more smirky smile, she was going to kiss it off his lips and then have to slap him again and realize that she had no self-control where this man was concerned. He was much more appetizing than Ghirardelli chocolate. She'd give up chocolate for life to keep kissing Bridger. *No! Be strong.*

Avalyn stormed past him, her dreams of relaxing at the pool and the beach completely shot.

"I rarely do what's good for me," Bridger said to her back.

Avalyn whirled around and glared at him. "Well, maybe you should start."

Bridger grinned. "You're the only thing that's good for me that I want, Ava Baby."

Avalyn gritted her teeth. He was wrong. She wouldn't be good for him. "You'd only want me until the next hot thing came along."

Bridger slowly crossed the distance between them, his eyes focused on hers. Avalyn couldn't drag herself away. Saints in heaven, she needed help!

He came so close she could smell his yummy, musky cologne and had to tilt her head back to meet his gaze instead of planting her face in his much-too-appetizing chest. He stopped and thankfully didn't touch her, or who knew how she'd resist kissing him. "If you'd be mine, I'd never notice another woman as long as I lived."

Avalyn's eyes widened. Bridger's mouth was set and his eyes were dark and determined. Was he being serious? If he was, it was the first and only time in his life. She studied him for too long. She needed to end this and make sure he stayed far away. "I'm a woman, not a possession," she shot at him.

Bridger's lips curved up in a smile. "Believe me, I know you're a woman." His gaze traveled over her face like a tender caress. It was almost as intoxicating as him touching her. "The most perfect woman in the world."

Just like that, Avalyn was panting for air again. What was he doing to her? *Be strong, be strong, he talks like this to every woman. He gives every woman his smoldering looks and perfect kisses.* As soon as Bridger got what he wanted from her, he'd move on so quick her heart would shatter and never recover.

"I will *never* be yours," she managed to push out. Her voice was trembling and the words weren't said nearly strong enough, but he finally got the message.

His dark eyes turned cool, and he easily slid back into that smirk that she loved and hated. "Never say never," he said.

"You can't have me," she said quickly, defensively.

Bridger's eyes slowly roved over her face, coming to rest on her lips for so long she was gasping for air again. If he kissed her, she didn't know how she'd resist, no matter how brave her words were.

"What's a challenge, and where do I find it?" he asked. It was his trademark line that he said quite often before performing some insane stunt that few athletes in the world could live through.

Avalyn gasped. He thought she was a challenge that he'd easily win. He thought he could obtain her. He was wrong. She whirled from him and stormed toward the nearest pool. Dropping her cover-up on a chair and sliding out of her flip-flops, she dove in, praying the cool water would cool the heat in her face—actually, the heat in her entire body.

She swam under the water, relishing its coolness rushing past her. When she finally had to surface for a breath, she popped up and gasped in the humid air. She only had today to enjoy a quick vacation before Creed and Kiera's sunrise wedding tomorrow morning on Christmas Eve. Then she'd fly home to spend Christmas Eve night and Christmas Day with her family and then back to work trying to bring healthy living conditions to the children of the world. Bridger Hawk could not ruin her one chance to rest and relax.

She blinked chlorine water out of her eyes and glanced across the pool. Bridger was standing at the edge, staring at her with a longing that made her stomach heat up again and the breath rush from her body. When he caught her gaze, he tilted his chin up and gave her another smirk before striding away.

He hadn't made it two steps before some girl in a bikini was squealing, "You're Bridger Hawk!" and asking him for a selfie. Bridger welcomed her with an open arm and a cocky grin. His eyes strayed to Avalyn, and his grin got even bigger when he realized she was watching them.

Ugh! Avalyn pushed back under the water. Somehow she had to stay far away from that man until she could fly away from here. It was either that or admit to him that she'd loved him her entire life.

# CHAPTER TWO

Bridger stood next to his three brothers as they waited for Creed's bride, Kiera, to start her march up the aisle. He was happy for his brother, who was finally marrying the love of his life. After everything he'd faced as a SEAL, Creed deserved some peace and happiness.

Bridger let his gaze stray to Avalyn Shaman. Sadly, the love of his own life loathed him. She met his gaze, and something raw and unguarded flashed in her deep brown eyes before she pressed her lips firmly together and looked away from him.

He didn't realize he was staring at her unabashedly until Emmett elbowed him in the side. "Be careful with Britney, eh?"

Britney? It was then that Bridger noticed the famous swimsuit model seated next to Avalyn. She was making eyes at Bridger as if he were staring at her, not Avalyn. Shoot. He'd been friendly with her the past few days—some might call it flirting—but it was simply a distraction to keep his mind off Avalyn, the way it was with every woman he flirted with and dated.

His brothers would cuss him up one side and down the other if they knew he only dated other women to try to push Avalyn out of his mind and heart. They'd say he wasn't being respectful of women or some such garbage. He was respectful. He treated women kindly, never offered any kind of commitment, and never did more than kiss said women. He'd hoped for years that he'd find someone that would push Avalyn out of his dreams. It hadn't happened yet, and those kisses yesterday morning had ruined him for at least another decade.

Kiera finally approached, and everyone stood as the bride's march song played. Bridger focused in on Avalyn again. She looked exquisite in a black dress that complemented her lean body, her long dark hair trailing across her smooth, brown shoulders. Bridger had seen many a beautiful woman in his day, but nobody compared to Avalyn. Her Middle Eastern heritage and philanthropist heart made her even more appealing. She was unique and perfect.

Why was she so determined to stay away from him? He'd acted much too impulsively kissing her like that yesterday, but she'd responded. Oh, how she had responded. The mere memory lit a fire inside of him. She met his gaze and stuck her tongue out at him. Bridger had to bite down a laugh, as this was a serious, beautiful moment for Creed and Kiera. Her dad was saying he gave this woman to Creed and all of that. Yet Bridger loved that Avalyn would tease with him. They'd been friends their entire lives, and he'd known she was the one for him since he was twelve and she was fourteen.

What was holding her back from loving him? He sighed and focused on the wedding. Maybe the fact that he'd never been worthy of her and never would be. What mere mortal could be worthy of Avalyn Shaman?

———

Avalyn's heart was slamming against her rib cage. Bridger kept giving her these heady, significant glances throughout the wedding. She needed to fly out of here as soon as social dictates would allow. Somehow she had to act cool and collected through the ceremony and the breakfast, and then she'd flee from Bridger and hopefully not see him again for a few more years. She'd pray hard for that miracle.

Creed and Kiera kissed, then held their joined hands high as everyone cheered. They walked happily down the aisle, and Britney Nolan, the supermodel, turned to Avalyn. They'd met last year at Emmett Hawk's fitness camp, where he'd asked Avalyn to be a guest speaker. Avalyn liked Britney.

"Wasn't that beautiful?" Britney dabbed at the corners of her eyes.

Avalyn nodded, cussing herself for not even noticing the beautiful ceremony; she'd been distracted by a more beautiful man.

They stood, and Britney linked their arms as they watched Emmett Hawk and Callum Hawk meet up with their respective fiancées, Cambree and Alexia. Bridger's parents were hugging, and Avalyn had that familiar feeling of being the only person without that special someone.

"Isn't he beautiful?" Britney murmured, gazing up to where Bridger was talking to the preacher, a young, smiling man who Avalyn had heard was one of Creed's Navy SEAL buddies.

"Yes, he is," Avalyn agreed, but she bit her tongue. She had to backtrack quickly. "The preacher? That's who you mean, right?"

Britney giggled. "The preacher's married and definitely not who either of us has been checking out." She sighed. "Aw,

Bridger Hawk. The only single Hawk brother left. Who do you think will claim that man's heart?"

Avalyn rolled her eyes at Britney's dramatics. "I don't think anyone can claim a heart as wild as Bridger's."

"Come on. I would think an independent successful woman like you would love a challenge like Bridger." Britney elevated an eyebrow. "Wouldn't it be fun to try to fight for him?"

"No!" Avalyn pulled in a calming breath. She was too transparent. Britney seemed to know exactly how Bridger was affecting Avalyn. *What's a challenge, and where do I find it?* She was not Bridger's challenge or anything else. If only she could keep her eyes from straying his direction every few seconds. "I know Bridger too well," she tried to explain to Britney. "He's a tease and a flirt, and I'm not in the market to be his flavor of the week."

Britney's smile deepened. "Well, I am. You're sure you're not into him? I respect you too much to go for your man."

"He is not my man!" Avalyn had to draw in another breath. The mere thought of Bridger being "her man" made her heart thump uncontrollably. Those stinking kisses yesterday. Dang him. "I promise. If you want him, he's all yours."

"Thank you." Britney was so beautiful, and when she smiled, it only enhanced her perfect face. Bridger would be thrilled to have her pursue him.

Why did that settle in Avalyn's stomach like a load of bricks?

"It's great to know you're not interested," Britney said.

"Not interested in what?" a deep voice said much too close to Avalyn.

She whirled to face the man of her every dream. Her tongue stopped working as she studied him in that perfectly cut navy-blue tux.

"You," Britney said. With a deep and throaty laugh, she released Avalyn's arm and put her hand on Bridger's chest.

Bridger glanced from Britney to Avalyn. "Why wouldn't you be interested in me?" His dark eyes bored into her, simultaneously offering a challenge and looking like a little boy who'd been hurt by a bully.

Avalyn still couldn't speak.

Britney laughed again. "She's the only one who's not, you stud, you."

Avalyn's eyes narrowed and jealousy rippled through her. No. She couldn't be taken down by petty thoughts like this. Bridger was an annoying little brother who she would never be compatible with, and she'd just given Britney permission to pursue him. "You've got him all to yourself, my beautiful friend. Bye." She forced a smile, which only Britney returned, and spun away. Striding through the sand in heels was no easy feat, but she plowed on.

A hand wrapped around her waist, lifting her clean off her feet. She glanced up, and again Bridger Hawk was much too close for comfort. His subtle musky cologne infiltrated her senses and she wanted to push him away, but she was rendered helpless as he carried her to the steps, then set her on her feet. When he released his grip on her, she could still feel the impression of his warm palm on her waist.

"Looked like you were struggling," Bridger murmured, his gaze dark and broody as he stared down at her.

"Thanks," Avalyn murmured, much too breathlessly. *Be strong, be strong.* "Where's Britney?"

Bridger inclined his head. "Emmett helped me out."

"Why would you need him to help you out? Go have fun with your swimsuit model." Avalyn felt guilty as she said that.

Britney was a nice person, and Avalyn would hate to be stereo-typed like that.

Bridger leaned closer to her. "Why wouldn't you be inter-ested in me?" He repeated the question from earlier.

Avalyn pushed out a breath, folding her arms across her chest. "You and I are never going to happen, Bridger." Why was he pursuing her so hard? They were family friends and she didn't want things to be awkward between them. She remembered those kisses from yesterday morning. Okay, too late on things not becoming awkward. Why had she allowed herself to respond to him like that?

*Because he's irresistible*, a little voice argued back.

"Why not?" he asked.

She rolled her eyes, praying for strength and the wisdom to explain so he would never try to kiss her again. If he did, she'd be sunk. "We're polar opposites, Bridge. You're a playboy who every woman adores. You don't take life seriously." The fact that he was crazy brave and could die at any moment while performing his stunts should be another reason to stay far away from him. "My life is dedicated to serious causes, helping the children of the world."

"I donate to your causes," he said.

"Throwing money at a cause is vastly different from living in the trenches and dedicating every spare hour of the day to it." She blinked at his hurt expression. What was this? She wasn't a guilt-ridden person, but she also didn't like to be the holier-than-thou type of person either. She'd made her choices for her life. She doubted Bridger could even understand the hours and days spent in primitive conditions helping and loving children. Her life was only occasionally glamorous and in the spotlight like

Bridger's. It didn't mean that Bridger's path was wrong; it just meant their paths couldn't coincide. "Thank you for donating. It makes a huge difference."

"But not enough of a difference," he murmured.

"To what?" Just like that, she was caught up in his gaze again. Why did he have to look at her like she was his whole world? She knew it was a lie, just an act he'd perfected to reel women in.

"To win your heart." His gaze pinned her in place as other wedding guests streamed around them on the stairs, heading up to the patio where the wedding breakfast was being held.

Avalyn backed away, clenching her hands together tightly. "You don't want my heart," she muttered.

"I want all of you, Ava." His beautiful brown eyes were framed by long lashes and dark brows, and right now they were studying her like she could make or break his life.

Avalyn's breath caught. She couldn't stay strong for one more second with him looking at her like that. Forget social protocol. She needed to get away, right now. She spun and hurried up the stairs.

A tinkling voice piped up from behind her. "There you are. Where are we sitting for breakfast?"

Britney. She could have Bridger. Britney was beautiful and kind, and Bridger would have a great time being around her. Britney had said she wanted to be his flavor of the week. Why that made Avalyn sick to her stomach was beyond her, but at least she didn't need to warn Britney that Bridger would move on to another woman tomorrow.

Avalyn strode toward the line forming to greet Creed and Kiera. She'd express her joy for them and get out of here, away from the pull Bridger Hawk produced every single moment he was around her. If she got far away from him, maybe she could think like a mature, accomplished woman and not a hormone-filled teenage girl.

# CHAPTER THREE

Bridger kept a bead on Avalyn as Britney led him up to congratulate Creed and Kiera and then dragged him along in the line for food. Britney was clingy and it made him uncomfortable, but then he noticed that Avalyn's gaze kept darting to them and he could feel the jealousy radiating off of her. It wasn't the intense love he dreamt of seeing from Avalyn, but maybe it was a step in that direction. If she was jealous, she must have some feelings for him, right?

Who was he kidding? Avalyn was the only woman he truly wanted, and the only woman who seemed impervious to his charms. Yet she had kissed him back yesterday. That fact alone gave him enough hope to keep praying for a chance with her.

He saw Avalyn talking to Lexi, Callum's fiancée, and thought the two of them would be fast friends. He liked all of his new and future sisters-in-law. How perfect would it be if Avalyn became close friends with Lexi like she already was with Kiera and Cambree?

Avalyn glanced his way as Britney's arms slid around him from behind. Avalyn's eyes narrowed, and Bridger shot her a grin and a raised eyebrow. *Come over here and claim me*, he hoped his look said.

She glared at him and turned back to Lexi. Dang. How was he going to shake Britney and get another go with Avalyn before she walked out of his life again? He'd rarely seen her over the past eight years, since she'd graduated high school and left them all behind. He'd only been sixteen, and of course she hadn't taken him seriously then. Her success and accomplishments made him proud and he knew she was out of his league, but why did she think they were so different? Every race, every crazy stunt he pulled was dedicated to some cause or charity. Everywhere he traveled, he tried to make a difference in the children's lives, even if it was just a smile, a hug, or a picture. Couldn't he and Avalyn change the world together?

Britney slid onto his lap, startling him. "Whoa," Bridger said. "You're making it a little hard to eat this delicious food."

Britney's lip came out in a pout. "I'll give you something more delicious."

Bridger chuckled, but his stomach soured. Britney was nice, underneath the innuendos. If Avalyn had said the same line to him, he'd be ecstatic. He'd dated women like Britney, but she wasn't his type, no matter what the media broadcast about him. Avalyn was his only type. He glanced back at where Avalyn and Lexi had been standing. They were gone. Panic fluttered inside him. They couldn't have left completely. Maybe they'd just gone to use the restroom or get more food. He strained to see the buffet table but didn't spot the dark flowing hair and perfect shape he would know anywhere.

"What's wrong, handsome?" Britney asked.

Bridger put his hands around her waist and lifted her onto her own chair. "Nothing. I'm just starving. Do you like yours?" He took a large bite of an egg casserole to prove his point. It was delicious.

Britney pushed her food around on her plate. "I can't eat like you and look like this." She gave him a forced smile.

Bridger wasn't sure what to say. He couldn't imagine the pressures she must deal with to have the perfect physique. It was interesting how Avalyn's shape was much more appealing when most of the world touted Britney Nolan as the most desirable body in existence.

"Have you done shoots here in Cancun before?" he asked, taking a bite of watermelon and hoping he could distract Britney from climbing onto his lap again.

"Oh, yeah, several times." She started talking about the different resorts, yachts, and adventure parks where she'd had professional pictures taken of her.

Bridger half listened as he ate and kept looking around for Avalyn. Maybe he should go look for her. No, that was stupid. She didn't want him around, and if he did find her, all she'd do was tell him off or slap him again. He'd have to store the memory of yesterday's kisses firmly in his mind. He doubted she'd ever let him have another taste of her perfect lips.

Emmett and Cambree strode up to them. Cambree's dark eyes looked troubled.

"Hey," Bridger greeted them. "Everything okay?"

Cambree nodded too vigorously. Then she shook her head, and her eyes brightened like she was going to cry. "Lexi left with Ava. They said they wanted to go home and be with their families for Christmas. Nothing is working out right! Have you seen Callum?"

Avalyn had really left? Bridger's stomach felt sick, and he wished he hadn't pounded his food so quickly. "He was going to California for a deal. I thought Lexi was waiting here for him."

Cambree lifted her shoulders. "I don't think she was too happy at being left behind."

Emmett wrapped his arm around Cambree's shoulders. "They'll work it out, love. You don't have to take care of everybody."

"Oh really?" She pushed at his chest. "And who do I have to take care of?"

"Only me." He bent down and kissed her.

Bridger had to look away. He didn't need to see another passionate display. It wasn't fun being the only Hawk brother left standing. If Avalyn would only give him some indicator, he'd be begging her to marry him. He rolled his eyes. Avalyn Shaman couldn't settle for a man who wasn't a superhero. Bridger shouldn't have kissed her like that yesterday, but she was just too irresistible to him.

"Aren't they cute?" Britney snuggled against his side. "Do you think you'll ever settle down, Bridger-boo?"

"Bridger-boo?" Emmett snorted. Apparently he was done with his public make-out session.

Britney grinned. Bridger needed to explain to her they weren't dating. Women always hated when he explained that he wasn't the guy to settle down, but they had to know it was inevitable. His reputation was to never have a relationship, even a short-term one.

Cambree steered Emmett away. "Have fun, you two. I'm going to try to find Lexi."

Fun? Bridger had fun when he leapt off a cliff in a wingsuit or executed a double backflip on a wakeboard. Sitting next to

Britney as she tried to corner him into something more intimate than he wanted was not any kind of fun in his book. He'd dug his own grave by flirting with her the past few days.

He forced a smile at Britney and wished there was more food on his plate to keep him from having to focus on her. Luckily, Creed's SEAL buddies started roasting his brother with their versions of toasting the groom. It was entertaining and almost distracted his mind and heart from the pain of Ava rejecting him yet again and leaving without saying goodbye.

Callum rushed up to him and Britney. Apparently he hadn't left for California yet. "Where's Lexi?" he demanded.

"Excuse me," Bridger muttered to Britney. He stood and walked away with Callum. "I saw her with Ava Baby."

"Where are they now?"

Bridger clenched his fists. "They didn't say anything to me, but Emmett and Cambree said they told them goodbye and that they were flying home to be with their families for Christmas."

"What?" Callum looked a little pale.

"Stupid woman anyway," Bridger muttered.

Callum grabbed a fistful of Bridger's shirt. "Don't you ever talk about Lexi like that."

"Lexi?" Bridger stared at him and then let out a dark laugh. He pushed Callum's hand away. "Not Lexi—Ava Baby."

"What is the deal with you and Ava?"

"Nothing." The muscles in his shoulders bunched around his ears. "No matter what I do, she barely gives me the time of day. I thought maybe Britney would make her jealous."

"Bro." Callum shook his head. "You're the one that has all the experience with women, but you're acting like a complete ... doofus." He smiled suddenly, looking like a doofus himself.

What had happened to his perfectly professional brother? A woman, that's what.

"A doofus?" Bridger glared at him. "You want to throw down right here?"

Callum rolled his eyes. "I haven't got time for this. I've got to find Lexi, but you need to listen up. Never use another woman to make a woman jealous. It's disrespectful to both of them. If you like Ava Baby ..." Callum paused and looked him over like he wasn't worthy of Avalyn. Bridger knew that was true. "Be a man and tell her."

Bridger stared at him. Hadn't he told her yesterday when he kissed her? But maybe he needed to really spell it out and keep the physical desires out of it so she knew it was from his heart. This wasn't some temporary crush. He'd loved her for as long as he'd known that boys and girls were different.

"I've got to go," Callum said impatiently. "Do you know what airport Ava's jet was at?"

"No clue, but I'll come with you."

"Let's go, then."

Bridger matched his brother's strides. It was a braver move than climbing Mt. Everest without assistance, but he was going to find Avalyn and he was going to tell her exactly how he felt about her. If she turned him down, then ... well, somehow he'd have to find a way to live with that.

# CHAPTER FOUR

Avalyn made it home to Long Island in time for Christmas Eve dinner. Her three older brothers had beautiful wives and six adorable children between them. She enjoyed being around everyone and shoved all the drama with Bridger to the back of her mind. Britney was probably thoroughly enjoying her Christmas with him. She liked Britney, but the image of her on Bridger's lap ... Ugh!

The adults had tucked the children into bed and set up the Santa presents, and they were enjoying Mama's homemade chocolates and talking when there was a pounding at the front door. Avalyn's parents did well financially, but they weren't to the level of the Hawks, and they didn't have round-the-clock staff. Avalyn preferred living that way; it was a lot more comfortable and intimate with just her family. Especially since most of her days were spent as a wanderer and a guest.

Avalyn's brother Abraham lumbered to his feet. "Don't worry. I got the door."

They all smiled. He was always rushing to do things or pay for things and then tell them not to worry because he had it. He was such a great guy. Avalyn hoped it was carolers or a neighbor visiting on this cozy Christmas Eve. She was glad she'd come home instead of staying in Cancun. The sun and the beach were fabulous, but nothing was like family and a warm fire at Christmas, and though she was still the only single one, it didn't hurt like it did watching the Hawk brothers' romances and having Bridger right there but completely unattainable for her.

Abraham sidled back into the room with none other than Bridger Hawk by his side. Avalyn's heart raced, and her palms started sweating. She couldn't quite comprehend Bridger being in her parents' living room like some perfect-looking ghost of Christmas past.

Bridger had come to Long Island instead of staying in sunny Cancun with Britney. Come for her? No. This had to be some mistake or crazy dream.

Bridger went around the room, shaking everyone's hands and being his usual charming self. Avalyn watched with her hand to her throat. Why was he here? Why? Why? He looked fabulous in dark gray chinos and a fitted long-sleeved shirt. His dark eyes sparkled as he teased with her family members. Why couldn't she just stare into those eyes as he teased with her?

He circled the room and finally stopped right in front of her. "Ava Baby." He gave her that irresistible smile, and she wanted to kiss him and smack him. She wasn't sure which one first.

"Why aren't you in Cancun with Britney?" She shot to her feet to face him.

Her family gave her confused looks. "Now, Ava, that's no way to greet your friend," her dad admonished her.

Avalyn didn't have the strength to pull her eyes from Bridger and explain to her dad that this man was no friend of hers.

Bridger reached out and took her hand. Avalyn's stomach tumbled. She should've pulled her hand free, but it felt so cozy and nestled perfectly in Bridger's larger palm.

"Would you excuse us for a moment?" he asked her parents.

Her mom's eyes lit up. Avalyn knew she'd prayed for most of Avalyn's life that she would marry a Hawk brother. Seeing how all the other ones were taken, this was probably a last-ditch hope for her mother. "Of course, Bridger. No one's in the study." Her mom gave him a warm smile.

Bridger guided Avalyn that direction with their hands clasped as if they were a couple or something. No. They weren't anything. The walk to the study seemed to take forever and pass too quickly at the same time. What was he doing here? What was he going to say? What if he kissed her again? How was she going to stay strong?

They walked into the room, which was softly lit with lamps and the glow of the gas fireplace. Bridger shut the double doors and guided her to a leather sofa. They sat side by side. She turned so she could see his handsome face and get a read on this situation.

"Why are you here?" she demanded.

Bridger squeezed her hand. "Ava." He took a slow breath and said, "I haven't seen you in years, before yesterday."

She acknowledged this with a lift of her chin.

He searched her face, his dark eyes warm, imploring. "Did the kiss yesterday mean anything to you?"

Her fingers involuntarily went to her lips. "You mean kisses?" she murmured.

Bridger smiled. "Yes, kisses." He leaned closer as if he would initiate that lovely sequence again.

Avalyn was in so much trouble right now. How could her family be a hundred feet away in the living room, oblivious to the current that threatened to sweep her away? Avalyn closed her eyes and prayed for strength. She opened her eyes and steeled her spine. "The kisses were ... very nice, but they didn't mean anything."

His brow furrowed. "I'm sorry to hear that, because I've never been so affected by any kiss."

Avalyn's eyes widened. Bridger was a smooth talker, but would he outright lie to her? The Bridger she'd known never would, but they'd hardly spoken since she'd left home at eighteen. She latched on to the way he'd phrased "any kiss." That was her out. His playboy ways. "You've kissed hundreds of women. Thousands! Don't try to act like I'm something special."

Bridger leaned closer. His breath brushed her cheek as he ran his hand along her jaw. "You are special, Ava. To me, there's no one as special as you."

Avalyn's breath caught. Oh, he was good. Too good. He was a professional playboy in every sense of the phrase. *Stay strong, stay strong.* "Why did you come here?" she demanded again.

"For you," he said as if the answer was that simple.

Avalyn pulled from his tender touch and stood. He slowly stood also, facing her. Every movement he made was glorious, sexy. But she didn't live her life for cheap thrills like Bridger Hawk. "I'm sorry you wasted a trip, Bridger, but you should go be with your family for Christmas."

He shook his head. "You don't understand, Ava Baby. I only want to be with you."

Avalyn backed up, clenching her hands behind her. "No. You

live for the challenge, Bridger Hawk. I am not your next conquest."

His eyes darkened, determination evident in every line of his face and body. "I live to succeed. I won't give up on you, Ava."

She wanted to scream, *Ha! Exactly!* He only wanted to succeed. It wasn't about her. It was about the fact that she had slapped him and told him not to kiss her. "Go back to your family and Britney. I'm sure she'd be thrilled to be your Christmas girlfriend." Even as she said the words, her stomach soured. She hated seeing Bridger with any other woman on his arm.

"I don't want Britney," he said in measured tones.

"Well, she wants you."

His eyebrow arched up. "And what does that mean? You don't want me?"

Avalyn jutted her chin out. "That's right. I don't."

Bridger's eyes swept over her carefully. Avalyn thought he might argue with her some more. The man didn't know how to lose, and she was more certain than ever that was the reason he was pursuing her.

"I'm sorry to have interrupted your Christmas Eve," he finally said.

Avalyn tilted her head, folding her arms across her chest so she didn't reach for him. "It was nice of you to stop by."

Bridger shot her his patented smirk, and its cold mockery was worse than a slap in the face. "Hopefully it won't be another eight years before I see you again."

Avalyn had no answer for that.

Bridger stormed through the study door. Avalyn followed him when she should've stayed safely in the study. He yanked the front door open. The cold air rushed in, but it wasn't nearly as cold as the look in his eyes as he glanced back at her. "Goodbye, Ava Baby."

Avalyn couldn't say goodbye. Not to him. He stared at her for a few beats, and she couldn't breathe as his dark eyes seared through her. Finally, he walked out into the crisp winter night. Avalyn pushed the door closed and leaned against it. Hopefully it would be longer than eight years, or she wouldn't survive the next encounter with Bridger Hawk.

# CHAPTER FIVE

Avalyn loved being with her family for Christmas break. Her nieces and nephews were the perfect distraction and almost kept her from pining away for Bridger. Almost. She still couldn't believe he'd followed her back to Long Island. It was insane and a bit surreal. She sometimes wondered if she'd imagined it all. Then one of her family members would tease her about dating Bridger Hawk, and she'd have to draw on all her acting skills from high school drama class to pretend she didn't care one bit about the man.

New Year's Day she said goodbye to everyone and flew to Belize City in one of Callum Hawk's private jets. He'd donated it to her foundation last year so she wouldn't have to deal with commercial flights. The Hawk brothers had given more to her and her causes than anyone in the world. Avalyn made decent money herself with the books she'd authored and the fees her agent negotiated when she spoke at various conferences, dinners, and auctions, but she couldn't have afforded a fraction of her humanitarian projects and especially not luxurious perks like her own jet and pilot without the Hawk brothers. They were good men. They just weren't the right men for her. At one point, she'd thought maybe she and Emmett would try dating—they attended enough benefits and auctions together—but there just wasn't any spark there. Why did there have to be spark with the crazy, youngest Hawk brother?

She exited the airplane with her suitcase in hand. A driver would be waiting and take her to the New Hope Orphanage. She'd start her visit there, but most of this trip was focused on outlying villages to assess the quality of nutrition and water and help teach the parents how to care for their children and keep them safe from diseases.

A driver waited by the airport exit with a sign with her name on it. She strode up to him.

"Avalyn Shaman?" he questioned with a slight Spanish accent.

"That's me."

He didn't smile, just gestured with his head. "This way, please." He reached for her bag, but she held on to it. He shrugged as if he'd tried.

Avalyn walked to the airport exit, but he put a hand on her elbow. "No, this way. Your agent made some changes to the trip."

Avalyn sighed, more annoyed than anything. She liked her agent, but the woman was much more bent on making money than giving it away like Avalyn was prone to do. She let the man direct her back through the airport and then out a side door. There was a helicopter ready. "What kind of publicity stunt does Sarah have planned?" she asked. "Are we not going to the orphanage first?"

He cracked his first smile. "No, ma'am." He wrapped his arm around her waist and pulled her against his side.

She tried to struggle free, but he was too big, too strong. Panic rose in her chest, making it impossible to catch a full breath. The annoyance she'd felt moments ago was crowded out by the rush of fear. What was this guy doing? There was no one around, but she screamed anyway, praying someone would hear and come help her.

He put a cloth over her nose and mouth. It was an odd-smelling mixture of sweet and chemical. Chloroform? Avalyn threw her head back but couldn't escape him or the cloth. As darkness edged in on her vision, she wondered who she'd ticked off this time and what they were going to do to her.

———

Bridger had finished a hard workout in the gym and was running sprints along the short length of beach in front of the resort in Cancun. He'd spent a nice week with his family. Luckily the wedding guests were mostly gone, especially one Britney Nolan, when he returned from New York, so he could just focus on his parents, his siblings, and their wives and fiancées. Callum and Lexi returned after a couple of days spent with her family. It was great to be with everyone, but by New Year's Day he was ready to throw himself out of an airplane without a chute.

He loved his family and they were fun and entertaining, but being without Avalyn was excruciating, especially when each of his brothers had a wife or fiancée by his side. Bridger was humiliated that he'd not only thrown himself at Avalyn repeatedly in Cancun but actually followed her back to Long Island, knocking on her parents' front door Christmas Eve. What kind of a loser did that? A desperate one, for sure.

He knew how unworthy he was of her, of course. Avalyn not

only noticed the discrepancy; she wasn't willing to bridge it. He didn't blame her, only mourned the fact that he'd never have a chance with her. He could only blame his desperate actions on his brothers being infected by the love virus, and he'd gotten all caught up in chasing his woman down like Callum was doing. It obviously worked out a lot better for Callum than him. He snorted. Why was he surprised? Everything worked out a lot better for Callum. The man was like Midas with his golden touch.

Bridger's phone rang, and he pulled it out of the pocket of his running shorts.

"Bridger," Ramsey greeted him warmly.

"Ramsey, my friend. How was Christmas?" He loved Ramsey. The guy had some screws loose, was even crazier than Bridger, but he was a lot of fun. The two of them were always competing for the number one and number two spots. Ramsey was constantly calling Bridger out on social media, doing some daring stunt and taunting that Bridger Hawk couldn't do it as well as him. Bridger hated to admit that he always rose to the bait, but he loved that he usually bested his longtime friend. Ramsey was a talented athlete, but he had a lot more money and power than common sense. Bridger guessed some people might say the same about him.

"It was great." But something in Ramsey's voice didn't sound great. "Lots of women, lots of sun. What more could you want for Christmas?"

Bridger grimaced. He only wanted one woman, and he couldn't have her.

"How was Creed's wedding?"

"Really great." How did Bridger tell Ramsey how badly he'd screwed things up with Avalyn? Ramsey had teased him about

Avalyn Shaman a few times throughout the years, but he doubted his friend recognized the depth and stupidity of Bridger's devotion.

"You up for a little friendly competition?"

"Always." His spirits lifted. He didn't care what Ramsey threw his way; this was his chance to get away from it all and forget about Avalyn, at least for a few seconds.

"I thought you'd say that."

"Name the time and the place."

"Fly into the Belize City airport. Text me your arrival time. I'll have my man meet you there. I'm finally going to beat you."

"You know it's hard being the best all the time. Maybe I'll let you win."

Ramsey laughed heartily. "I love you, man, but you've never let me win. I think you'll want to trash me on this one."

"I always want to trash you." Lately Bridger felt like he was slowing down, tiring of their never-ending competition, all the cheap thrills, the media, the parties. Yet risking his life for a stupid adventure and YouTube video might be the only way he could stop thinking about Avalyn.

# CHAPTER SIX

Bridger took Callum's Airbus down to Belize, a short half-hour flight, and then sent the pilot back. His brother was great to him. Bridger usually just chartered planes or boats. He had plenty of resources, investments, and sponsors but he wasn't interested in owning the world, just conquering it.

In the airport, he spotted a burly, bald guy in a suit holding a piece of card stock with Bridger's name on it. Bridger approached him and inclined his chin. "You my ride?"

"Yes, sir."

"Bridger Hawk." Bridger extended his hand.

"Mike." The man returned his handshake with a crushing grip.

Mike tilted his bald head toward a different airport exit. Bridger followed him. A chopper was waiting. He carried his bag himself; the guy hadn't offered, and Bridger didn't care about pomp and service.

They climbed into the chopper. Bridger greeted the pilot,

who simply nodded to him. Another burly guy was waiting for him inside. "Ramsey expecting me to put up a fight?" Bridger joked.

Mike cracked a grin as he shut the door and the chopper took off. "He said you could take us both down, so we shouldn't start anything."

Bridger smiled too. "Aw, that warms my heart." His internal radar was pinging strangely. He and Ramsey had been friends for a long time. They teased and tormented each other like brothers. Why the security presence?

"You know what the competition is?" Bridger asked.

"No, sir."

Bridger nodded. He wasn't getting anything more from this guy. He pulled out his phone. Might as well delete emails and deal with sponsorships and questions from his agent while they flew.

He was halfway through an email to Under Armour when Mike yanked the phone from his hand, tossed it on the floor, and ground it under his boot heel.

Bridger cursed and jumped to his feet. "What was that all about?"

The guy simply stared at him and inclined his head. "We're here, sir."

Bridger looked out the window, his stomach churning with anger. Had Ramsey told this idiot to shatter his phone? Why would his friend do that? Bridger wanted to take the guy out, but he'd save it for the thick-necked, thick-skulled idiot's boss.

Ramsey's massive white yacht waited below. Bridger had been on the yacht for parties several times. The pilot expertly descended and settled the bird onto the landing pad on the top.

Mike shoved the door open and gestured. "After you, sir."

Bridger shook his head. "My fist and your face are meeting soon, dude."

The guy smiled and pulled out a semi-automatic rifle. "He told me you could take us down, but you don't want a bullet in your skull, now do you?"

Bridger's stomach rolled. He and Ramsey had competed for years and definitely both wanted to be the alpha, but they were friends and they respected each other. It'd never gotten weird or violent. What was going on?

———

Avalyn had awoken with a huge headache, lying on a soft bed. She started breathing hard and fast, her stomach churning with fear. Why had she been kidnapped? Neither she nor her family made enough money for it to be about ransom. Maybe because she was associated with the Hawks? No, that would be stupid. They'd kidnap Kiera, Lexi, or Cambree, not just a friend of the family. She'd ticked somebody off, then. That was the worst-case scenario, because it meant they'd want to hurt her or try to make her stop working on one of her causes.

She pushed herself off the bed with a groan. The windows were all drawn in the room, but it was a decent-sized suite with a table and chairs, a sofa, and the king-sized bed. She could see a bathroom through one of the doors. Everything was high-quality. The floor rocked slightly. It must've been the aftereffects of the chloroform.

She padded to the closest window with her hand on her head, willing it to stop pounding. She pushed the shade up and gazed out. Sunshine sparkled off water for as far as she could see. Her stomach clenched as more fear poured over her. Someone had gone to a lot of effort to kidnap her, and they obviously had money. The possibility of escaping a world of water wasn't very encouraging. No wonder everything was rocking. She took some deep breaths, telling herself not to borrow trouble. Soon enough she'd know what she was up against. But she had nothing to bargain with. Nothing but her brain and her iron will.

She heard the distinctive whir of helicopter blades, and at the same time, her door burst open. Two large men with guns strode into her room. "Miss Shaman," one said by way of greeting. He gestured with his gun out into the hallway.

Tilting her chin up, Avalyn marched in front of them down a wood-paneled hallway and into a large gathering area. Everything was pristine with tan leather seating, gleaming wood, metal accents, and lots of windows looking over the ocean. The water was a true blue, so she was probably still in the Caribbean, but there was little hope of anyone finding her out here. If anyone was even looking. Her pilot and stewardess didn't expect her until the end of the week. Her family had said goodbye for the month of January. The director of the orphanage in Belize might contact her agent and start a search, but there were no guarantees of that. What she wouldn't give to be kicking a soccer ball around with the children right now.

"Wait here, please," the man said.

"What do you want with me?"

The man gave her a big grin and a wink. "Oh, I wouldn't mind a lot with you, ma'am, but it's my boss who will have some answers for you."

She shot him an imperious glare, not appreciating the way he looked her over. "Take me to him."

"Patience, my beautiful lady."

The other guy suddenly grabbed her, whipped her away from

him, and pulled her hands behind her back. Avalyn cried out and tried to struggle free, but he was too strong. She kicked back at him and heard a grunt as the heel of her tennis shoe connected with his leg. He held her tighter, and the first man bound her hands with zip ties.

Avalyn's terror whipped into a frenzy as another man appeared from a different hallway, carrying a heavy anchor. "What are you doing?" she cried out. "Stay away from me!"

He simply smiled and knelt down next to her. She kicked at him, but he easily dodged it. The first man held her upper body while the second wrapped his arms tightly around her legs. The third man secured a rope to her ankle that attached to the anchor. They were going to drown her. She pulled in and pushed out breaths, teetering on the edge of hyperventilation.

# CHAPTER SEVEN

Bridger jumped out of the helicopter, leaving his bag—the idiot could put it in his room. He strode down the first set of stairs he saw, toward the main deck. The two burly guys followed close on his heels. He noticed Mike was carrying his bag.

Ramsey reclined on a cushioned chair on the main patio. He opened his eyes as Bridger strode up to him. Languidly, he stuck his hand out. "Bridger, my friend. You made it."

Bridger batted his hand aside, seconds away from throwing punches. "What's going on, Ramsey? Your dude shattered my phone."

"Ah, now." Ramsey stood and spread his hands innocently. He looked like a jaguar with smooth, lean muscles, too-tanned skin, and a silky smile. The women loved him almost as much as they loved Bridger. "I couldn't have your Navy SEAL brother tracking us, now, could I?"

Bridger straightened. Everything felt off, and he could sense danger all around. He glanced at his nine o'clock to see two more men strolling up, each toting guns that meant business. The guys from the helicopter were behind him, and two more men sauntered out of a glass door at his three o'clock with their own huge weapons. "What is all of this?" Bridger's throat was dry and his abdomen tight. He could fight his way out of any situation, but not when bullets were involved. Unfortunately, he was mortal.

"I have a little surprise for you, my friend." Ramsey wrapped an arm around his shoulders.

Bridger shrugged him off. "I haven't liked your surprises much today," he spit back. Ramsey was a nut job, and Bridger had the feeling he'd underestimated the amount of crazy bouncing around in Ramsey's head.

"Well, you're going to love this one. Shane," he hollered, "bring the woman."

Woman? Bridger's stomach took flight. What woman had Ramsey involved in whatever he was planning?

Two men came out the sliding glass door, hauling a woman in a black fitted shirt and yoga pants. Her beautiful dark hair spilled down her back.

"Ramsey, no!" Bridger yelled, hurrying toward her.

Guns cocked all around him, stopping him in his tracks.

Avalyn lifted her head and pinned him with a glare. "You're involved in this?" Her eyes were wide and filled with fear and loathing.

Bridger shook his head, holding his hands up. "Ava, I ..."

"Ah, this is beautiful." Ramsey clapped his hands a few times. "I hoped I would find the woman Bridger Hawk loved desperately, and it appears I've chosen correctly."

Bridger blinked at the bright sunlight and Avalyn's angry

glare. He needed to play this right if Avalyn had any chance of escaping unscathed. For some reason, Ramsey had snapped. Too much money? Too many drugs? Who knew? But his friend definitely wasn't acting friendly today.

Bridger forced a laugh. "So, what, this is some fun publicity stunt? We should get a lot of attention and new followers. Maybe even some new sponsors with Avalyn Shaman involved."

"I refuse to be part of your stupid publicity stunt," Avalyn said. She looked glorious with her dark eyes sparking fire at him, standing tall and unafraid, even as she had her hands bound behind her and ... why was there an anchor tied to her ankle? His heart thudded faster and faster. "And if you wanted the woman he loved, you should've kidnapped Britney Nolan, not me."

Bridger couldn't believe that he was worried about contradicting Avalyn. Ramsey had definitely gone off the deep end. No wonder he'd ground Bridger's phone to dust.

Ramsey pursed his lips. "The supermodel? Yeah, she would've been a lot of fun." He sidled over to Avalyn and walked a circle around her, his eyes traveling over her body in the fitted clothing.

Bridger's fists clenched. Could he kill Ramsey before his men filled him full of bullets? Nobody but Bridger could look at Avalyn like that.

"No. I think you'll be the perfect motivator for our boy here. I've watched him. Whenever anyone mentions Avalyn Shaman, he lights up like a Christmas tree." He sneered. "And I need him to have the proper motivation to make this stunt work. I'll have so many people following my YouTube Channel, I'll be more famous than any of the Hawk brothers." He ran his hand down her cheek.

"Don't touch her!" Bridger yelled. He started forward again.

A man stepped in his path and pushed his gun into Bridger's chest. "Where do you want me to shoot him, sir?"

Ramsey smiled. The smile was familiar, but there was something in his eyes Bridger had never seen before. Obviously he didn't know his friend as well as he thought he did. "We can't kill him ... yet. But a bullet in his arm would slow him down and help me win the competition." Ramsey walked away from Avalyn and up to Bridger. "And I think you'll want to win this competition. The winner of each round ... gets to spend the night with Avalyn Shaman."

Bridger froze for a second. His heart thundered in his chest. Was Ramsey serious? What made him think he could use Avalyn like this? The gun jabbed harder into Bridger's chest, and ice trickled through his veins. It appeared Ramsey was more than serious.

Bridger glared at him. He could beat Ramsey any day, but Ramsey was right that the motivation of protecting Avalyn would make him up his game. He still was having trouble processing that Ramsey would threaten Avalyn like this and tell his man to shoot him. Bridger had no clue what was going on with a man he'd considered a friend, but he couldn't afford a bullet right now. If Ramsey somehow won ... He couldn't stand to imagine what his former friend would do to Avalyn. Ramsey loved a lot of women, and he didn't stop at kissing like Bridger did.

"Nobody wins me," Avalyn snapped at him.

Ramsey arched an eyebrow at her. "You have no control here, Miss Shaman. I suggest you shut that pretty mouth."

"Don't talk to her like that," Bridger ground out.

Ramsey laughed. "I can see that you two haven't figured out yet that I'm in charge. I guess the eight automatic weapons pointed at your heart isn't proof enough. How about the fact that we're in the middle of the Caribbean Sea with no help in sight and both of your phones have been shattered and sunk in the sea?" He smiled. "But soon enough you'll feel real fear and you'll know who's in charge."

Bridger had felt more fear since the man had dragged Avalyn out onto the deck than he had his entire life. No death-defying stunt was as terrifying as the woman he loved being in this psycho's power. The scariest part was that Bridger had no clue what Ramsey's plan might be.

Ramsey must be bipolar or something to be acting so insane. Bridger prayed the Ramsey he thought he knew would show up, start laughing, and explain he'd just wanted to get their reactions, scare them for a minute. As he looked into Ramsey's eyes, he had the sinking feeling that his prayers wouldn't be answered.

————

The mercenaries stood quietly next to Avalyn for a few moments. No one said anything to her or tried to touch her again. Two more men walked past them with huge weapons in their hands. They didn't so much as glance at Avalyn as they walked out the wide glass doors at the rear of the gathering area. Avalyn saw more men out there and could hear voices, but she couldn't make out the words. One lone man had his back to her, but she could've sworn it was Bridger. Oh my, she was grasping at hope right now. Bridger wouldn't be here with these criminals.

A few seconds later, two of the men grasped her arms and tugged her toward the glass door; the third man picked up the anchor and struggled behind them. The men on the back deck all spun to face her as they exited the cabin, and she gasped. It *was* Bridger. Bridger was here! He would protect her. Hope fluttered in her chest, but then it sank. Could Bridger be one of them?

"Ramsey, no!" Bridger yelled, hurrying toward her.

Guns cocked all around him, one man shoving his weapon into Bridger's chest, stopping him in his tracks.

Avalyn glared at the man she thought she loved. "You're involved in this?" Fear made her throat dry and scratchy. Bridger wouldn't let them drown her in the ocean, would he?

Bridger shook his head, holding his hands up. "Ava, I ..."

"Ah, this is beautiful." Another man clapped his hands a few times. "I hoped I would find the woman Bridger Hawk loved desperately, and it appears I've chosen correctly."

Bridger blinked at her, and then his lips turned up in a smirk and he laughed. What was the jerk laughing about? "So, what, this is some fun publicity stunt?" He looked to the man who was clearly in charge. Ramsey. She'd seen him in Bridger's YouTube videos before; they always bantered and competed. The man reeked of too much sun-tanning and too much money. "We should get a lot of attention and new followers," Bridger continued. "Maybe even some new sponsors with Avalyn Shaman involved."

"I refuse to be part of your stupid publicity stunt," Avalyn said. A publicity stunt sounded better than being drowned, though. Her heart was shredding inside her. Bridger! The man she'd thought she loved would use her for a publicity stunt? "And if you wanted the woman he loved, you should've kidnapped Britney Nolan, not me."

Bridger simply stared at her.

Ramsey's eyes widened. "The supermodel? Yeah, she would've been a lot of fun." He strolled up to Avalyn and walked a circle around her, his eyes traveling over her body in her T-shirt and yoga pants. The clothes she'd been traveling in. She wanted to scream that she wasn't some bimbo to eye like a snack. "No. I think you'll be the perfect motivator for our boy here. I've watched him. Whenever anyone mentions Avalyn Shaman, he lights up like a Christmas tree."

Avalyn's heart started pounding fast for other reasons. Bridger had made his intentions pretty clear last week, but the thought of him "loving her desperately" made her want to throw herself into his arms. No. He was a playboy jerk, and this just confirmed it. Using her and her name for publicity, putting her in this horrible situation for more followers? What a slime.

Ramsey sneered. "And I need him to have the proper motivation to make this stunt work. I'll have so many people following my YouTube Channel, I'll be more famous than any of the Hawk brothers." He ran his hand down her cheek. Avalyn flinched away from him.

"Don't touch her!" Bridger yelled. He started forward again. A man stepped in his path and pushed his gun into Bridger's chest.

"No," Avalyn breathed. Maybe Bridger was a pawn in this too. She should've been terrified, not hopeful, that Bridger wasn't one of them.

"Where do you want me to shoot him, sir?"

Ramsey smiled. "We can't kill him ... yet. But a bullet in his arm would slow him down and help me win the competition." Ramsey sauntered away from Avalyn and up to Bridger. "And I think you'll want to win this competition. The winner each round ... gets to spend the night with Avalyn Shaman."

"Nobody wins me," Avalyn shot at him, horror racing through her. She would never be with a man like Ramsey. The mere thought made her want to throw herself off the yacht and take her chances with the sharks. Instead, she stood straighter and glared at him, pretending he was a politician trying to tell her she couldn't help children because of their stupid and ever-present red tape.

Ramsey arched an eyebrow at her. "You have no control here, Miss Shaman. I suggest you shut that pretty mouth."

Avalyn strained against the men holding her.

"Don't talk to her like that," Bridger ground out.

Ramsey laughed. "I can see that you two haven't figured out yet that I'm in charge. I guess the eight automatic weapons pointed at your heart isn't proof enough. How about the fact that we're in the middle of the Caribbean Sea with no help in sight and both of your phones have been shattered and sunk in the sea?" He smiled. "But soon enough you'll feel real fear and you'll know who's in charge."

Avalyn couldn't imagine what more fear she could feel. Already she was close to hysterics, passing out, or hyperventilating. How had she gotten involved in this nightmare? Was it just because this Ramsey guy thought Bridger loved her, or was there something deeper? Bridger may have wanted her, but he didn't love her. She wasn't sure Bridger Hawk was capable of real love. Sadly, that was the least of her concerns at the moment.

The thugs manhandled her toward the back deck of the boat. The yacht wasn't moving, so at least she wouldn't be sucked into a motor when they pushed her overboard, but the hope of swimming with her arms secured behind her back and an anchor tied to her ankle were pretty much shot. *Please help me, Lord*, she pled in her mind.

Bridger hurried after them. "Ramsey, don't do this," he demanded. The men stopped at the edge, and Bridger reached for her. He got pushed back by the wrong end of an assault rifle. He held up his hands and beseeched the men. "She's innocent. Please don't do this."

Ramsey approached them on the back deck, sauntering along like they were walking on the beach.

"Ramsey." Bridger turned to him, holding out his hands. "Come on, man, we're friends."

"Best of friends." Ramsey grinned.

Avalyn's stomach dropped. Ramsey was Bridger's friend? What kind of monster had his thugs point guns at his friend?

"Don't do this to her," Bridger begged.

She had never seen Bridger beg, for anything. Even as a child or young teen, she'd seen his brothers teasing, sometimes torturing him, and he'd just smirk and yell at them to bring it on. Her heart twisted and expanded toward him at this moment. She was going to die and Bridger would do anything to protect her. Sadly, with all the armed men and the psychotic Ramsey, protecting her might be impossible.

"Come on, man. I'll do any publicity stunt. I'll lose to make you look good. Anything you want." Bridger's voice dropped low. "Please don't hurt her."

Ramsey grinned. "I knew I'd found the perfect woman. Let the games begin."

Then he shoved Avalyn into the water.

"Ava!" Bridger yelled.

Avalyn's instinct was to scream, but luckily she clamped her mouth tight and held her breath. She flailed, but the anchor on her ankle dragged her down fast. Pressure built in her head until she thought it would explode. She tried not to breathe in and speed her demise.

She stopped descending suddenly. The anchor must have hit

the bottom of the ocean. She'd done free dives and scuba dives many times, and the instructor always claimed that if you slowly blew bubbles out, you could hold your breath longer. She tried, she really tried, but darkness edged in on her vision and the need to breathe in was all-consuming. She prayed to the Lord above for a miracle as she struggled to push the rope off with her other foot and somehow contort her body to get her hands to her ankle and free herself.

Bridger. Would he come for her? Could he save her?

# CHAPTER EIGHT

"Ava!" Bridger screamed as Avalyn was shoved off the boat deck and quickly sank in the clear, blue water. Ramsey had gone insane! Bridger ripped off his shirt and kicked off his shoes.

Arms grabbed him from behind and held tight. "Calm down, man," said Ramsey's voice. "You've got to give her time to sink."

Bridger elbowed the guy holding him and was rewarded with his elbow making contact with his fleshy nose, a scream, and one of his arms was released. The guy holding his other arm clung tight. Ramsey was grinning and cameras were rolling. Bridger was going to kill Ramsey ... right after he rescued Avalyn.

"You gotta say your line or we can't let you go after her," Ramsey said.

Bridger's eyes narrowed. He didn't care about his stupid line, but he growled, "What's a challenge, and where do I find it?" Then he reached out and grabbed Ramsey, slamming him into the man clinging to Bridger's arm. They both howled in pain, and finally Bridger was free.

He dove into the water, angling his body straight down. The water was so clear he could see Avalyn probably forty feet down on the ocean bed. At least Ramsey had anchored at a shallow spot so Bridger had a chance of saving her. He'd covered maybe half of the distance when he saw a dark shadow approaching. Ramsey was diving much faster than Bridger was, holding on to a heavy rock.

Bridger angled toward him, knocking his former friend off course and ripping the stone from his hands. He dropped much quicker now, his ears popping and his head close to exploding. He had gone deeper on a free dive, but forty feet was plenty to feel the pressure and pain, though thankfully without the risk of the bends when you surfaced.

At least Bridger would be the first one to reach her, so there was no risk of Ramsey claiming he got to stay with Avalyn tonight. What a nasty jerk to even put that on the table. Bridger would protect her virtue, if he could get her out of the water before they both died. He dropped the rock to the side, horror slicing through him as he saw that Avalyn had passed out. *Please don't let her die*, he begged his Father above.

He tugged at the rope on her ankle, working the knot frantically. It was too tight, pulled even tighter by her being dragged to the ocean floor and the water sealing it in place. No! He grabbed the rock he'd dropped and tried to chisel through the rope with the sharp edge. He was running out of oxygen and his lungs felt like they were being crushed. He blew out bubbles slowly. *Please, Lord. Help me!*

A shadow blotted out the sunlight above. Bridger glared up at Ramsey. If the man didn't help Bridger save Avalyn, he was going to kill him with his bare hands and hope they posted it on YouTube.

Ramsey held out a knife. Bridger ripped it from him and quickly cut through the rope tying Avalyn's ankle to the anchor. As soon as it gave, he released the knife, pulled Avalyn into his arms, and kicked for the surface. There was no time for any kind of slow ascent. He'd built up a tolerance for dives like this and would be fine, but what would it do to Avalyn? Her body was horribly limp. He could see Ramsey out of his peripheral vision and two other bodies as well, both in full scuba gear with camera equipment. If they'd had men down there, why didn't they help? Ramsey was truly insane.

Bridger's head burst through the surface. He was twenty yards from the yacht, and he dragged her that direction. Ramsey surfaced and helped him. Men reached down and lifted her onto the back of the platform. A man started CPR immediately.

Bridger launched himself onto the boat. He pushed at the man's shoulder. "Let me," he demanded.

The man glared up at him. "I'm a trained paramedic."

"Oh." Bridger fell back and waited with bated breath. The sun beat down on him, drying the water on his skin. Despite the tropical heat, he was chilled to the bone.

Ramsey climbed up onto the platform, also eyeing Avalyn with apprehension. Bridger couldn't wait to take him out; he didn't care how many weapons were aimed at them. He'd use Ramsey's body as a shield from the bullets as he pummeled him with his fists. But first he had to know Avalyn was okay. She lay there motionless as the man kept breathing into her nose and mouth. *Please, Lord, please.* Bridger was a religious person and had good communication with the Lord above, but he couldn't ever remember praying so diligently.

He met Ramsey's gaze across Avalyn's unresponsive body. Ramsey's eyes were full of remorse and concern. Bridger didn't care. Ramsey had better be praying Avalyn lived, or Bridger would drown him. The weapons couldn't stop him under the water.

The only sounds were the water lapping against the boat and the paramedic's movements as he finished chest compressions and went back to rescue breathing.

With a sudden gurgle, Avalyn threw up sea water.

Bridger's breath rushed out of him. She was alive! The paramedic pushed her onto her side, and she heaved out another rush of water before just lying there, trembling.

Bridger wanted to swoop her up and get her far away from this nightmare, from these men who would have killed her for a publicity stunt. He stormed toward Ramsey. "You could've killed her!"

An arm encircled his throat and a gun was shoved into his abdomen. Another man came at him from the other side with another gun aimed at his chest. Bridger wanted to throw them off and pummel Ramsey, but he'd be no help to Avalyn if he was dead.

"You were the one who could've killed her." Ramsey stalked toward him. "I have this all planned out. She will be perfectly safe if you'll stop going off half-cocked."

"What are you talking about?"

"You would've had your own weight and knife to get to her and to cut her free if you didn't freak out and go all rogue! It was supposed to be a level competition."

"This woman is not the object of your crazy competition." He gestured to Avalyn. She looked so fragile and innocent, curled on her side. He'd never seen Avalyn helpless, and it tore at him. He wanted her to sit up and put them all in their place with her usual commanding and inspiring presence. The paramedic guy wrapped a blanket over her abdomen and legs and talked quietly to her. Avalyn's eyes were closed, but he could see her shoulders shaking.

"I'm afraid she is." Ramsey glared at him. "You have yourself to blame for endangering her today. This will be a fun competition, if you'll just trust me."

Trust him? "Give me that knife now; I know just where I'll put it." Bridger struggled to free himself from the men pinning him between them. The guns were jammed harder into his abdomen.

Ramsey laughed, but it was shaky. Was he really committed to going through with his insane plan after seeing Avalyn almost die? "Come on, my friend. Calm down. You won't be any help to her if I give them permission to fire."

Ramsey was no friend of his. Bridger didn't know if they'd truly shoot him if he fought, but it took all of his strength to stand down. How could he get Avalyn away from all of this? Maybe if they were posting the videos each day, Creed would be able to find them, track their progress, search out Ramsey's money trail, something.

"Tomorrow you need to slow down and listen to instructions, not fight your way through like you do with everything. This is a friendly competition, man. Make it fun." Ramsey winked as if they were competing at the world surf championship and it was all good fun.

"No tomorrow, Ramsey. You have your crazy video. Use it however you want, and let us go."

Ramsey smiled patiently, spreading his hands. "I'm afraid that's not going to happen. I've got days and days of events planned out. And in case you have any high hopes that one of your big brothers will save you, know that I'm not going to start posting the videos until the competition is over and you two are stored away at a secure facility." His eyes gleamed. "If you survive." He clapped his hands. "Now. I'm exhausted. Would you like to join me for dinner, or would you like to have your dinner in Miss Shaman's suite with her?"

Bridger drew in a ragged breath. He saw no way to fight ten armed men and escape in the middle of the ocean. "We'll eat alone," he muttered.

"Ah, I'd choose the same. Enjoy your night with her, Bridge. Tomorrow night she might be mine." Ramsey walked away, chuckling.

Bridger's jaw clenched. He would never let Ramsey have his way with Avalyn. He'd die first.

The men released him, and he hurried to Avalyn. She sat up as he approached, and the blanket slid down on her shoulders. Her clothes and hair were plastered to her. "Bridger?" she whispered, gazing up at him with her beautiful dark eyes, looking much too uncertain and afraid.

His chest tightened. He'd almost lost her today. How could he get her far away from Ramsey? He couldn't imagine the gauntlet of activities Ramsey had planned. The man claimed he wouldn't hurt Avalyn, but she could've easily died today, and doing any of the extreme sports they usually did could result in death or serious injury. Especially if she was tied up.

He bent low and swept her into his arms. Having her close was settling, though anger at Ramsey still traced through him.

The men stood back out of their way, except for Mike, the baldy who'd met him at the airport. "Her room is this way, sir."

Bridger jerked his chin up at him and followed the man

through the spacious living area and kitchen and down one of the hallways. Mike pushed open a door, and Bridger strode inside, slamming the door closed behind him and securing the lock with one hand as he clung to Avalyn with the other. It was silly, as the men could bust in here at any moment. No lock could keep Avalyn safe.

Despair overwhelmed him. How was he going to protect her every day? What if Ramsey won and she was forced to spend the night with that slimeball? What if neither of them won and she died in one of these stupid adventures? Bridger had been an extreme athlete for years now, but he suddenly had no stomach for adventure or thrills. He wanted to be tucked away in a quiet house in Long Island with Avalyn cuddled in his arms. Their parents just down the road. Maybe a baby on the way. If that dream could come true, he would give up all this insanity.

Sadly, it was a dream that he couldn't make come true. Even if they escaped, Avalyn had made it abundantly clear on Christmas Eve that she didn't want him. He held her close. At least she was in his arms and safe ... for the moment.

# CHAPTER NINE

Avalyn couldn't stop shivering. A coughing spell racked her body. When it settled, she stared up at Bridger's handsome face. She was alive. Had Bridger saved her? He must have, or else she'd be in the horrid Ramsey's arms. A shudder passed through her.

Bridger's brow furrowed. "Oh, Ava Baby. I'm so sorry."

She pushed out a breath, and her gaze settled on his bare chest. She let herself lean her cheek against the smooth skin and muscle, too spent to pretend she didn't want him to simply hold her close until all the fear went away. "You're sorry," she muttered. "Because you saved me?" She glanced up at him.

A muscle worked in Bridger's jaw. "Ramsey only brought you here because of me."

Avalyn's breath caught. This Ramsey guy really thought Bridger loved her? Maybe in this twisted world these people lived in, Bridger's version of love 'em and leave 'em would be considered devotion. That wasn't her world. How was she going to get out of here? Her chest tightened and she started coughing again. Her head hurt worse than it had when she'd awoken from being drugged earlier.

Bridger carried her through the room into the attached bath. He set her on her feet and pulled open the glass shower door, pulling the shower knob out. "We've got to get you warm."

Warm sounded wonderful. The ocean hadn't been cold when she'd first fallen in, but maybe a near drowning just made you feel cold all over. Bridger tested the water with his hand and then turned to her. He grasped the edges of her shirt and started to lift it.

"Bridger!" Avalyn cried out, pushing his hands away.

"What?" His dark eyes were confused as he focused on her face.

"You aren't undressing me," she said sharply. Did he undress women regularly? The mere thought of it consumed her with jealousy.

"Oh!" Bridger was close enough that she could feel the heat radiating from his body. His hands settled on her waist. "I ... was just trying to help."

"Well, I don't need your help."

Bridger stared down at her. His eyes were so full of concern and worry for her, it about broke her resolve to keep him at arm's length. "I don't want to leave you," he murmured, his gaze traveling over her face.

Avalyn pushed out an unsteady laugh. The worry over other women was pushed far away as she basked in Bridger staring at her as if she were something special to him. "Yeah, well, you're going to have to," she murmured. "At least so I can shower."

Bridger stepped back, and Avalyn felt like she could breathe again. How could she have all these romantic thoughts when she'd almost died and Ramsey was going to try to kill her again tomorrow? Bridger was only this attentive to her because she had nearly drowned and there were no models and actresses around to compete for his affection.

"You'll be okay?" Bridger asked, averting his gaze from her.

"Yes, thank you."

He nodded. "Wait a second. I'll grab your suitcase." He hurried from the bathroom and returned with her suitcase. Without another word, he set it down next to the vanity, then stepped back out of the bathroom and shut the door tight.

Avalyn pulled in a slow breath, her hands still trembling from cold or shock, she wasn't sure. She peeled off her wet, salt-water-caked clothes and hung them over the glass shower door to drip-dry. She retrieved some shampoo, conditioner, and body wash from her suitcase. It was surreal to do something as normal as showering when they were in this horrific situation, but as she stepped into the warm water, she couldn't help but send up a prayer of gratitude. They had survived, and Bridger was here with her. For some reason, he gave her strength to think she could face tomorrow.

———

Bridger paced outside the bathroom door while Avalyn showered, prepared to go in there if he heard a crash or bang of any sort. She had to be a mess right now and he hated leaving her alone, but he needed to respect her privacy, and if he saw her in the shower ... well, all of the self-control his parents had instilled in him and he'd maintained throughout the years would probably fly out the window at that point.

A rap came from the hallway. He hurried over and opened

the door. Mike handed over his bag. Then he gestured, and a younger man walked in with trays of food on a rolling cart. It smelled delicious. The young man nodded to him and walked back out. Mike stood by the door, rubbing his bald head.

"Thanks." Bridger started to shut the door.

Mike put his hand on it. "You did good today, man."

Bridger stared at him, not sure what to make of the compliment. "Thank you."

"Is Miss Shaman ... okay?"

Bridger shrugged. "As good as she can be."

Mike opened his mouth, but then he closed it. He nodded once before turning and striding back down the hallway.

Bridger shut and locked the door, then returned to his post by the bathroom door. It was torture to think of Avalyn showering in there, but he pushed his longing far away. He couldn't get distracted by wanting to hold her or kiss her. He had to play Ramsey's games and save her each day until they could escape.

What was up with Ramsey? Bridger still couldn't wrap his mind around this twisted competition Ramsey had created. The moment Ramsey had shoved Avalyn into the ocean, with an anchor tied to her ankle, kept replaying over and over in his mind. Would Ramsey really do something that malicious to gain more followers? Not the Ramsey he'd thought he knew.

The shower stopped, and still Bridger waited. Quite a while later, the bathroom door swung open and Avalyn appeared with a mist of steam. She looked fresh and beautiful with her long hair wet and smooth down her back, wearing a simple white sundress. Her dark skin contrasted so perfectly, he wanted nothing more than to run his fingers along her smooth shoulder and reassure himself that she was all right.

"Have you been standing out here this whole time?" She planted her hands on her hips and tossed her hair.

Bridger couldn't help but smile. "Had to make sure you were okay."

The teasing light in her dark eyes went out. "I'll be fine."

It was fake bravado, but he was proud of her for it. She was Avalyn Shaman, and nobody was going to conquer her. At least, he hoped not. "I'm going to shower quick," he told her.

She nodded, her shoulders straight and her chin tilted at a proud angle. "I'll be fine while you shower, Bridge. I'm not a helpless female."

"I know that, it's just ..."

She met his gaze. "We're in a horrid situation. I know. Shower quick."

He gave her a smile, grateful she wanted him close by, and then rushed into the bathroom and shut the door behind him. It smelled like vanilla cupcakes, and he felt heat rush through him. Why did she have to look so good and smell so good? He rushed through his shower and within minutes was pulling on some gray shorts and a white T-shirt.

He hurried out of the bathroom door. Avalyn was curled on her side on the bed. Her body trembled as she sobbed.

"Oh, Ava," he murmured. He hurried to her side.

She sat up, brushing angrily at the tears.

"I'm fine. You were too quick."

Bridger laughed in surprise. She was so tough and brave. He shouldn't have been surprised by how well she was dealing with this nightmare; she was one of the most impressive and independent people he knew. It just made him fall for her even harder.

"You are not fine." He sat down on the bed and pulled her against his chest. Thankfully, she didn't resist. She laid her head against his shoulder, and Bridger knew he could conquer anything for this woman, but for the first time in his life, he didn't want to conquer. He wanted to get her far away from here and hold her like this until she tired of him.

Avalyn's arms wrapped around his waist and she clung to him. Bridger trailed his fingers along her back.

After much too short of a time, she gazed up at him, her dark eyes bright with more tears. "What do you think he's going to do to me tomorrow?" she whispered.

Bridger's breath caught. He hadn't let himself go there. "I don't know." Her eyes were so full of fear it ripped at him. "But Ramsey doesn't want you to die."

She blinked at him. "You're insane. I think he only wants to hurt you, and he thinks by killing me—or close to it—he can accomplish that."

Bridger didn't know what Ramsey's motivation was. Until a few hours ago, he'd thought they were friends. Yes, they competed fiercely and Ramsey always wanted to beat him, but to want to kill the woman Bridger loved? That was insane, even for Ramsey. How Ramsey knew Avalyn was the woman of Bridger's dreams was beyond him. They'd spent a lot of time together competing and at parties after competitions, but Bridger didn't realize he was so transparent when it came to Avalyn.

"It shook him up when you weren't breathing," he said. "He brought me the knife to cut you free and helped me pull you back to the yacht. He had a paramedic there to help. I think this truly is about publicity and a fun time for him, plus he would love to best me." He shuddered just thinking about that, imagining if Ramsey won. Avalyn would be in Ramsey's arms instead of his.

He forced himself to release her and stand, extending his

hand. "Let's eat dinner and let them get good and high—Ramsey drinks or drugs out most nights. Then we'll sneak out of here and find a way off this ship." The lack of women on this ship disturbed him. Ramsey loved women, and he loved partying. Who would he party with? His bodyguards? Something was really off, and Bridger had no clue how to get to the bottom of it.

Avalyn took Bridger's hand and let him lead her to the table and the cart full of food. He uncovered the trays, and the scents of steak and freshly made bread floated out. His stomach rumbled. So weird he could be hungry in the midst of all of this, but he hadn't eaten since this morning in Cancun. This day felt like it had stretched forever, and he didn't like the thought of facing tomorrow and Ramsey's next challenge. They had to get out of here.

"How are we going to do that?" Avalyn asked, taking the plate he offered and filling it with some salad and steak carbonara.

"The helicopter we came in on is still here, and if I can't find keys or hot-wire it, there will be rescue boats or sometimes even a speedboat on a yacht this size. The rescue boats would be equipped with emergency sensors. See? Lots of options." He gave her a brave smile but wasn't feeling as hopeful as he tried to pretend. Ramsey might be a cocky druggie, but he was also a brilliant and successful businessman. The chances of him leaving Bridger an opportunity to escape were one in a million.

# CHAPTER TEN

A valyn tried to act normal—well, as normal as a person could act knowing they'd most likely die in the morning —as she and Bridger ate dinner and then waited for the yacht to settle down. They talked about their families and all of his new sisters-in-law and which projects her charity Health for All was working on.

She told him a story about a darling little girl who had been scratching Avalyn's back with a pen during a long church meeting in Cebu, Philippines. Neither of them had realized the pen had been clicked on, and Avalyn's white shirt was covered with blue pen marks. The girl had looked up at her when her mom scolded her and asked hopefully, "Miss Shaman, do you have another shirt?" Avalyn laughed again as she told the story, though it still tore at her that having another nice shirt for church was a novel thing for the child.

She enjoyed talking to Bridger, but there was an underlying strain with the fear of what may come, the gratitude that they'd survived this day, and the desire to come out and ask him if Ramsey was right and she was the love of Bridger's life. He looked at her like he cared deeply for her, but Bridger Hawk wasn't capable of a lasting relationship and Avalyn couldn't settle for a shallow hookup. She loved him far too much and would never recover.

It had been dark for a couple of hours, and the only sounds were the water lapping against the side of the boat. As they'd eaten dinner, the yacht had started moving, which terrified Avalyn even more. They were on their way to the spot for the next extreme event that could result in her death, or her being left alone with Ramsey for the night. She wasn't sure which was worse. She'd rather join the angels in heaven than be defiled by the likes of Ramsey. He was truly a twisted and evil person.

Bridger inclined his head toward the door, and her stomach clenched. This was it. If the good Lord above was watching over them, they'd find a way to escape, but the thought of creeping around the quiet yacht looking for that out and praying they didn't run into Ramsey or one of his gun-toting lackeys didn't seem very likely. She just wanted to get back to the children and off this insane yacht. She loved the little ones, and every time they gave her a smile or clasped her hand, it made the long hours she put in to bring them clean water, food, and healthcare all worth it.

Bridger took her hand and they crept toward the door. He paused and listened, then unclicked the lock, pushed the handle, and pushed the door open.

Two men stood at the door, aiming their scary-looking guns in Bridger and Avalyn's faces. The taller one smiled. "We were placing bets on how long until you tried to escape." He tilted his head to the other guy. "You owe me a hundred bucks."

The other guy chuckled, but his grip on the gun stayed steady. "Double or nothing? You know he's gonna try again."

Bridger nodded to them. "Put your guns down and I'll bet you a thousand bucks I can kick both your butts."

Avalyn clutched his hand tighter. She hated violence, but at the moment she would've loved to watch Bridger knock them both out.

The tall guy's eyebrows drew together. "That sounds really appealing, but Ramsey pays us far more than that."

"I'm worth a lot more than Ramsey," Bridger said, as confident as ever. "You help us escape and I'll give you any dollar figure you ask for."

Yes! Avalyn hadn't thought of that. Maybe these hired mercenaries could be bought.

The men exchanged a look as if they were considering it. Finally, the taller one spoke again. "As appealing as that sounds, and as big of a fan of yours as I am, there's no way to escape. Ramsey made it pretty clear. The helicopter's buttoned up tight, as is the speedboat, and the lifeboats have been disabled. He knows you too well, sir."

Bridger studied him. "So you want to help us?"

No one spoke.

"What's your name?" Bridger asked.

"You can call me Klein."

"Please help us, Klein. You saw what happened today. Ramsey's gone crazy. He might kill Avalyn tomorrow. She spends her life helping children throughout the world. You can help save her."

The other guy focused on Klein.

Klein's eyes flickered to Avalyn, and she felt hope for the first time today. Just as quickly, the man's jaw tightened and he pushed the gun up against Bridger's shoulder. "You will find that every guard here is committed to Ramsey and cannot be bought or reasoned with."

Just like that, Avalyn's stomach dropped. She swayed and leaned against Bridger. He stood tall and strong like their one hope of escape hadn't just been terminated.

"Our instructions are to maim you, sir, not kill you," Klein continued. "If you force me to do that, who's going to rescue Miss Shaman tomorrow?" His eyes filled with a darkness that terrified Avalyn. "You're his friend. You know what Ramsey is capable of with women."

"Was his friend," Bridger muttered.

Avalyn's breath caught in her throat. She clung to Bridger's hand. Escape wasn't going to happen, and if Ramsey bested Bridger, how would she defend herself from him? She'd taken some self-defense courses in college. Would they be enough? As she remembered Ramsey's glistening strength, she feared they wouldn't be.

"Please get some rest. Your best hope is to run his gauntlet."

Slowly, Bridger nodded and tugged Avalyn back into the room. He closed and locked the door.

Avalyn's body trembled, and she bit at her lip to hold back the sob that was working its way up her throat. They would never escape from the psychotic Ramsey. Even though his men were sympathetic to their plight, they wouldn't help them.

She'd been in a village in Africa last month that had been decimated by human traffickers. Some of the children had been recovered, but hopelessness and fear still lurked in their eyes. She'd been sympathetic but had no way to empathize, until now. Being helpless and in an evil person's power could easily strip a person of their will to thrive.

Bridger gave her a forced smile. "You take the bed. I'll sleep on the couch."

Avalyn's breath was coming too fast. She clung to Bridger's hand and begged, "Please just hold me."

Bridger's eyes darkened. He looked her over with such desire and tenderness it made breathing even more difficult. He didn't say anything, just walked with her to the bed. Slipping off his shirt and his shoes, he turned the bed down and waited while she slid off her sandals and climbed in, still wearing her sundress.

He climbed in after her, wrapping his strong arms around her and cradling her against his chest like a priceless artifact. She wanted him to hold her tighter, but she'd take whatever strength she could glean from him. *Bridger is strong. He'll protect me.* She repeated those words over and over again.

Bridger brushed his lips across her forehead. "It'll be okay, Ava," he whispered. "It'll be okay."

Avalyn knew he couldn't assure that, but his confidence and his strength flowed into her. They hadn't escaped, and they probably wouldn't. Tomorrow loomed terrifying and much too close, but Bridger would protect her. She had to believe that or she'd crumble completely.

# CHAPTER ELEVEN

Avalyn woke to the sun streaming across the bed through the blind she'd left open yesterday afternoon. Bridger's beautifully formed arms were still wrapped around her back so she was cuddled into his chest. She could hardly believe she'd slept, but now, all the fears of last night resurfaced a hundredfold. Her breathing came faster and faster.

Bridger's arms tightened around her. "It's okay, Ava. Calm down, just calm down."

Avalyn tried to listen. She tried to focus on his muscular chest pressed close to her. She tried to pray. Nothing helped.

"Breathe with me," he murmured, his breath warm against her forehead. "In." She could feel his chest expand. "And out." He kept repeating "in and out," and she followed his breathing technique. Gradually, her body relaxed and she felt like she wouldn't hyperventilate.

Bridger scooted back a little bit and brushed the hair from her face. He smiled down at her. "You're so brave and beautiful."

She stared at him. He was the picture of strength and bravery. "I feel like a complete mess," she admitted. She'd never felt so helpless and unsure of her future. She was always in control, always doing for others. Right now, she could only think about her own miserable doom.

"So do I."

Her eyes widened at his admission.

"But we'll get through it together."

Together. Avalyn didn't know that she and Bridger could ever truly be together, but she needed him. She'd never needed a man like she needed Bridger. Not just to protect her during the challenges, but to hold her, to breathe with her, to make her smile when there seemed to be no reason to smile.

"Do you trust me, Ava?" His gaze held her captive.

Avalyn swallowed, not sure how to answer. She trusted him to protect her, to give his life for her if necessary, but she still didn't trust him with her heart. She didn't know that she ever could. "I trust you to protect me," she finally said.

Bridger's gaze sharpened. He knew what she was holding back, and he didn't like it.

A rap came at the door, and then the lock turned and the door opened. "Mr. Hawk? Miss Shaman?"

Bridger released her and sat up. Avalyn followed his lead, sitting up in the bed and staring at the guards, different men than the ones they'd confronted last night. A young man rolled in a tray of food.

"Thank you," Bridger said, standing.

One of the guards nodded. "After you eat, please get dressed in comfortable clothes and make sure you wear socks and shoes."

"Okay."

They all walked out, shutting and locking the door behind them.

Avalyn stood and stretched. She wanted to shower and then sleep for another few hours in Bridger's arms again, if possible. She shook her head; she was getting way too invested in him. He was an amazing man and he was here for her now, but she knew nothing would last beyond this nightmare, if they ever escaped from it.

She felt eyes on her and glanced at Bridger. He was staring unabashedly at her. When she met his gaze, he averted his and gestured toward the food.

Avalyn followed his lead and sat at the table. Her stomach tumbled from the apprehension of the day. Last night in the dark, safe in Bridger's arms, she could somewhat push today away, but now it was here. She tried to think about the children, wonder what Sadie, who ran the orphanage she was supposed to be at in Belize, was doing with the children right now. Maybe serving them breakfast, helping the older ones get ready for school. Sadly, Avalyn's mind returned quickly to the terror from yesterday as Ramsey had pushed her off the yacht.

Bridger claimed Ramsey didn't want to kill her, that he'd brought a knife to cut her loose in the ocean and helped Bridger get her back to the yacht. She didn't know if she believed that, and she knew all about the risks of extreme sports. Her Bridger obsession had led her to research the chances of death and injury in each of the sports he participated in. It had been sobering and terrifying, another reason she tried to not fall in love with the man. And now she was thrust in the middle of those alarming statistics. Even worse, she was relying on someone else to save her.

She picked at her eggs and fruit while Bridger scarfed down

an omelet, toast, and a banana and drank several glasses of milk. "How can you eat?" she asked.

Bridger looked at her, his dark eyes filled with concern. "I'm going to need all my strength."

She swallowed hard and looked away.

Bridger stood and then dropped to his knees next to her. He grabbed both of her hands in his. Avalyn's breath popped out of her. He looked so handsome and intense as he studied her. She'd never seen Bridger serious like he'd been last night and this morning. "I won't let him have you, Ava," he said, "and I won't let you die."

Avalyn bit at her lip. She felt like some queen whose best knight was promising to give his all for her. But Bridger was so much more to her than any loyal subject. She wanted to kiss him, which was insane. Who had time for kissing and thoughts of love when they were in the middle of a nightmare like this?

Bridger's gaze brimmed with determination and a deep commitment to her. Was it possible Bridger might truly love her? Love her even beyond Ramsey's insane challenges? Her heart expanded and ached to let him in at the same time.

The door lock clicked and then swung open. The guard cleared his throat. "It's time."

Bridger studied her for a few more beats, then stood and pulled her up with him. "You can get dressed in the bathroom."

She nodded and hurried into the bathroom, shutting the door behind her and leaning against it as she tried to catch her breath. Her heart was in as much danger from Bridger as it was from death. Normally, Bridger was hilarious and carefree; right now, he was serious and focused on protecting her. She'd never seen this side of him, and though she hated the circumstances, she liked knowing that he could and would rise to the occasion when it was necessary. Yet if they ever made it back to the real world, would he simply go back to his playboy ways? She liked his sense of humor, but not his lack of commitment and his disregard for his own safety.

She forced herself to open her suitcase and pull out a sports bra, a neoprene T-shirt, and some running tights. She slid into them and put on socks and running shoes. Then she brushed the taste of the eggs off her teeth and secured her long hair in a ponytail. She didn't waste time on makeup, not caring if she looked good for Ramsey's stupid video.

When she opened the door, Bridger was waiting in a fitted T-shirt and cotton shorts. He extended his hand to her, giving her a forced smile. She walked to him, wanting to be strong, but the tension inside her and around them grew with each second. Yesterday she'd almost drowned. What did Ramsey have planned today? She blocked it out. If she allowed herself to think about it, she'd crumple to the floor and sob.

She took Bridger's hand, his warm fingers surrounding hers, giving her the security she needed to put one foot in front of the other and keep her spine straight.

"You look like my dream woman," Bridger murmured. "Have you met her?"

Avalyn laughed. "What?"

Bridger gave her the infuriating smirk that had always drawn her in. "Yeah, her name's Avalyn Shaman, but I like to call her Ava Baby."

Avalyn shook her head at him, grateful he could still tease and somewhat distract her from their impending doom.

They followed the guards down the hallway, through the main areas, and outside. A tropical island rose out of the water maybe a quarter mile away. They ascended the stairs, the whir of the helicopter blades growing louder and louder. Avalyn's stomach churned. She enjoyed being in the water, and look how horrific yesterday had turned out. She was absolutely terrified of heights. Maybe they were flying to that island for some kind of challenge. She prayed desperately, *Please let it be better than yesterday*. She had to trust Bridger and he'd said he didn't think Ramsey wanted her dead. It sure felt like he did, though.

Bridger helped Avalyn into the helicopter. Ramsey was waiting in a seat, grinning at them. The helicopter door shut behind them, and Avalyn glanced around at the four guards and the pilot.

"Welcome." Ramsey spread his hands wide. "Take a seat."

They obeyed, strapping lap belts on. The helicopter rose into the sky, and Avalyn's stomach took flight with it.

"You're going to love today."

"What I love and what you love are very different," Avalyn said.

Ramsey chuckled. "Obviously. You love Bridger Hawk." He wrinkled his nose. "Me, not so much."

How did Ramsey know she loved Bridger? Was she that transparent?

Bridger held on to her hand, looking pointedly at Ramsey. "Call this craziness off, Ramsey. You'll never get away with it. You'll be hunted down by the U.S. Government, the U.N., my brothers, Sutton Smith ..."

Ramsey's grin grew. "Will I, now?"

Bridger glared at him. "Come on, Ramsey. You don't want a repeat of yesterday."

Avalyn shuddered.

"Let's do a competition," Bridger continued. "You and I. Anything you want. Just leave Avalyn out of it."

Ramsey's blue eyes focused on her. "But then I wouldn't get the chance to spend the night with her."

Avalyn's heart dropped to her stomach. The only thing worse than dying would be spending an entire night at Ramsey's mercy.

"You will *never* spend the night with her," Bridger growled, his hand tightening around hers.

"Never say never, my friend." Ramsey threw back his head and laughed. "Isn't that your line? Never say never." He stood. "We ready?"

"Yes, sir," the pilot said.

The guards threw the door open and wind rushed in. *No, no, no.* Avalyn looked around wildly. The island was far below them. She could barely make out the ridges of mountains and the sandy beaches touching the blue water.

Two of the guards set down their weapons and strapped on parachutes, then picked up camera equipment. The other two guards ripped Bridger away from her. Avalyn screamed.

Bridger fought wildly. He kicked and clawed and punched. Just as Avalyn hoped he might get free, she felt hands grab each of her arms and rush her to the edge. She looked out at blue nothingness. The men pulled her feet out from under her and they all plunged out of the plane.

"Bridger!" Avalyn screamed, stomach acid clawing at her throat.

Then the men released her and she was free-falling through the air, her body being flung around. She screamed and her stomach dropped like the worst horror ride she'd ever been on. She tried to see the helicopter and Bridger coming for her, but it was only blue sky and then the island below, blue sky and then the island below. The island was rushing up to meet her much too fast, and her head and stomach were spinning. The roar of the wind in her ears added to the terror.

She was going to die. She'd never feel Bridger's arms around her again, never bask in his smile. Why hadn't she just kissed him last night? She closed her eyes shut tight and prayed desperately, *Let Bridger catch me. Please let Bridger catch me.*

# CHAPTER TWELVE

Bridger fought to free himself from Ramsey's ugly thugs. He landed a solid punch to one's abdomen, then kicked the other. He was almost free when the two other guards sandwiched Avalyn between them and leapt from the plane.

"No!" he screamed. His arms were released and he rushed for the door, looking down as the guards released Avalyn and her body twisted in an out-of-control free fall.

Ramsey grabbed his arm and shoved a parachute at him. "Let's do this buddy."

Bridger hated Ramsey more than he'd ever hated anyone in his life. He hurried to strap the parachute on. Ramsey leapt a second before him. Bridger dove out of the plane, angling his body straight at Avalyn. Ramsey couldn't get there first.

He could hear Avalyn's screams being carried by the wind draft, and it tore at him. He prayed and he tried to focus, streamline his body, and dive quicker. Ramsey was just in front of him and they were closing in on Avalyn fast. The ground was rushing up faster. Would they be able to catch her and pull the chute in time? The thought of Ramsey touching her couldn't take a back seat to saving Avalyn's life.

Bridger couldn't let him win, though. Avalyn's virtue was too important to him. They were feet from Avalyn when Bridger grabbed Ramsey's foot and yanked him the other direction. Ramsey hollered out.

Bridger slammed into Avalyn, wrapping his hands tight around her arm. She cried out in pain.

"I've got you!" he yelled, clinging to her arm. He tried to maneuver her around in front of him. The ground was probably only a thousand feet away now. They had to pull the chute, but she'd be ripped from him if he didn't secure her.

"Pull it," Ramsey yelled, and from the corner of Bridger's eye, he saw Ramsey's chute deploy.

"Ava!" Bridger commanded. "Turn toward me and hold on." He tugged at her, and she wrapped one leg around the back of his thigh and clung to his waist. "Hold on!" He ripped the chute cord.

The parachute blasted out above them and they jerked. Ava screamed as her grip around his waist slipped. Bridger held tightly to her arm. He wrapped his other arm around her waist and held her snug against his body. Her body trembled against him, and he imagined he was trembling worse. But he had her. He'd caught her and he'd beaten Ramsey to her.

The peaceful silence that always came after traveling at terminal velocity didn't calm him down like usual. The ground was coming up too fast. He yelled, "You gotta hold on tight to me!"

Avalyn obeyed, clinging to his neck with her arms, both of her legs now wrapped tightly around his lower back. Bridger grabbed the chute handles and directed their descent toward the beach. Hitting the sand or the shallow water would be much better than getting caught in the tropical forest or slamming into a rock. It looked like a dozen men were on the ground waiting for them. Ramsey was just above him to his right.

Bridger landed on the sand, trying to run with the momentum, but Avalyn's weight against him threw him forward. They hit the sand hard and rolled together, getting tangled up in the chute. But they were alive and Ramsey hadn't won.

Bridger lay there with Avalyn clinging to him. He tilted her chin up so he could look in her eyes. "You okay?"

She nodded bravely.

He could hear men's voices, and the parachute was cut away.

Avalyn stared at him as if he were a hero or something. Then she leaned in and kissed him right on the lips. Bridger savored the warmth of her lips. Sparks seemed to light the humid air around them. She pulled back much too quickly. "Thank you," she breathed out.

"The kiss was more than enough thanks." Bridger gave her a confident wink, but inside he was reeling. The terrifying game of catching Avalyn took a back seat, for a moment, to her kiss. Avalyn Shaman had willingly kissed him. He had to remind himself it was in the middle of an intense, crazy situation, so he couldn't place any value on it, but he wanted to shove the men away who were trying to help them to their feet and continue that kiss. Dared he hope she was changing her mind about him? Would she ever give them a chance?

Mike helped him out of the chute and clapped him on the shoulder. "You did it. Great job!"

Bridger acknowledged his praise with a chin lift, unsure how else to respond. This wasn't some athletic event. The woman he loved had almost died, again.

"Whoo-hoo!" Ramsey yelled out. Men helped him out of his chute and he jogged across the sand to them. "What a ride! And you win again. Good job, brother."

Bridger couldn't take it anymore. This man was not his brother. He stepped up to pummel the guy, but Avalyn dodged in front of him and slugged Ramsey in the gut. Ramsey grunted, surprise registering in his blue eyes.

"You're a psychotic monster!" she screamed in his face.

Ramsey laughed as his men lifted their guns and pointed them straight at Avalyn. He waved them off. "It's okay. I deserved that. You guys got lunch set up? I'm starving." Ramsey slapped Bridger's shoulder on his way past; Bridger pushed his hand away. "Good times, man." He chuckled and strutted off.

Bridger pivoted after him, but several rifles pushed into his face made him stop.

The tall guy from last night, Klein, was behind one of the guns. He nodded to Bridger. "Good jump, sir. Lunch is this way."

Bridger pulled in a ragged breath. He turned and wrapped his arm around Avalyn's shoulders. She was still trembling. They walked slowly in front of the guards up the beach to where some tables and chairs and a small lunch buffet was set up. Bridger looked around and could see the speedboat anchored in a shallow bay. The helicopter had landed in a clearing a little bit away.

He bent down close to Avalyn's ear. "You okay?" he whispered.

She looked up at him, her dark eyes full of admiration. "Thanks to you."

He needed to lighten the moment. "So I'm getting a lot more kisses later? To say thank you, I mean."

She laughed, but then her eyes sobered. "I don't give out my kisses easily, Bridger Hawk."

Bridger's stomach dropped as he realized what she was implying. He'd kissed hundreds of girls. He couldn't even remember most of their names. Yet if Avalyn would commit to kissing him for life, he'd never be tempted by any other woman. "Lucky me, then." He gave her a smirk.

She lifted her eyebrows. "Hopefully your luck hasn't run out."

Bridger lost all humor as that statement hit him. His luck of getting a kiss from Avalyn, or his luck of saving her life and protecting her from Ramsey? He needed the luck of the Irish right now, but he'd keep praying and rely on blessings from above. Thinking of that, he said a silent prayer of gratitude that they'd survived another round.

———

Avalyn made it through lunch without slugging Ramsey again, but only barely. He joked like they were all friends and laughed at Bridger's dark, sarcastic comments about Ramsey's mental instability and lack of sense.

After lunch, Ramsey jumped up. "You two up for a hike? You have to see the waterfall. It's only a couple of miles each way."

Avalyn glanced at Bridger. He shrugged at her. Avalyn loved hiking and especially waterfalls, but she hated this twisted reality Ramsey had trapped them in. He wanted to challenge Bridger and almost kill Avalyn every day, then pretend they were all friends who ate a delicious lunch on the beach and went for a hike after? What kind of a monster did that?

"I ... yeah, I like waterfalls," she admitted.

Ramsey clapped his hands together. "Let's go, then." He nodded to his men. "Thanks for everything, guys. Who's coming with us on the hike?"

Avalyn and Bridger exchanged a look. These men looked and acted like mercenaries, yet Klein had told Bridger last night that they were all committed to Ramsey. Why? He treated them like his friends, but there was a deeper reason that eluded her.

Most of the men followed them up the trail past the beach. No one said much as they walked through the lush jungle. Avalyn focused on the beauty of the thick trees and birds twittering around, not allowing herself to think about her freefall an hour ago and what Ramsey might be scheming for tomorrow. She did let herself think about that moment when Bridger had caught her. Even though they'd still been plunging through the air, she'd felt safe. He was her personal hero. An amazingly tough and handsome hero.

A stream trickled past them on their right. Vines hung down around it from the huge trees. She'd been in a lot of tropical places and was always amazed how the people in such areas could survive on very little and were so happy without worldly possessions. They'd fish for their dinner, pluck a mango off a tree for their breakfast, and get their water from the stream. Their focus was on relationships. Avalyn was in so many different areas of the world that she didn't develop deep relationships often. What could she and Bridger develop if she let down her guard with him? Would it last beyond this nightmare with Ramsey?

The trail was barely wide enough for one person. Ramsey led the way, with Avalyn directly behind him. Avalyn appreciated the opportunity to be in nature and move her legs. It helped calm the anxiety over her impending doom. Bridger was walking behind her. She glanced over her shoulder, and he gave her a reassuring smile and a wink. Avalyn smiled back.

How could he make her feel so special and safe when there was no reason to feel either? She knew she couldn't be special to a man who would never settle down with one woman, and she was the furthest thing from safe—walking directly behind Bridger were men with guns strapped to their backs, and not because they were worried about animals in this remote jungle. They were worried about Bridger attacking their boss, and with good reason. It warmed Avalyn clear through that Bridger wanted to take Ramsey out for her.

Water pounding against rocks reverberated throughout the forest. Ramsey glanced over his shoulder at her, his blue eyes lit up. If Avalyn didn't know he was a murderous psycho, she'd think he was a fun-loving, happy guy. She'd seen him in different videos of Bridger's and always thought he was funny and seemed like a good guy. How wrong perceptions could be.

"Do you like to swim in waterfalls?" Ramsey asked.

"Yeah," she said slowly. Who didn't like to swim in waterfalls?

"You're going to love this."

Bridger's hand rested on her back, as if to assure her he was there and she wouldn't be subject to Ramsey. He kept it there as they crossed the last fifty yards and then entered a small clearing.

She stared up at the beautiful waterfall dancing over mossy rocks. It wasn't as powerful as some she'd seen, but it was very pretty as it pranced from one boulder to the next before doing a freefall descent forty feet to a clear pool beneath. The water from the pool trickled out and down the stream they'd been walking next to.

Ramsey ripped off his shirt and climbed up the boulders next to the waterfall. It was a precarious climb, but he moved like a mountain goat. When he was about sixty feet up, he yelled, "Watch this!" and pushed off and dove into the pool below.

"Is that pool deep enough?" Avalyn gasped out. Then she shook her head. She shouldn't care if Ramsey split his skull open.

He surfaced, beaming at them. "Try it!"

Avalyn shook her head. "No thanks. I'm afraid of heights."

Ramsey's face blanched. Avalyn wondered if he actually felt remorse, if he was even capable of it. He seemed like he had multiple personalities or maybe was bipolar.

He swam to the edge of the pool and stood, the water about waist deep. His tanned body glistened with water droplets. Avalyn supposed most women would consider him attractive. Not her. His mouth worked, and he finally said, "Good thing we're done with the parachuting, then."

Bridger wrapped his hand around her waist as Avalyn's stomach churned.

"You'll do it, won't you, Bridge?" Ramsey asked, like an eager child.

"He really needs to find some friends," Bridger murmured to her.

Avalyn hid a laugh.

The guards stood stoically, not taking off their shirts to swim. Their faces were impassive. She supposed Bridger was right. If these were Ramsey's usual companions, he desperately needed some real friends. Maybe that was why he was so crazy.

Avalyn hoped Bridger wouldn't do the jump. If he got hurt, who knew what Ramsey would do to her? She could see him eyeing it as if he wanted to jump.

"We'll just swim," Bridger said.

Avalyn's eyes widened. Bridger had turned down a quick

thrill. For her?

"Aw, c'mon. Bridger Hawk never turns down a challenge," Ramsey taunted him. "'What's a challenge, and where do I find it?' That's the Bridger Hawk we all know and love."

Bridger tensed against her. He ignored Ramsey and looked to Avalyn. "Do you want to swim?"

She nodded. She did want to swim, but the pool wasn't very big and she didn't want to be anywhere near Ramsey.

"Come on in." Ramsey splashed some water at them, a gleam in his eyes. He pushed his way out of the water and sat on a rock.

Bridger directed her around the pool, twenty feet from where Ramsey sat. He let go of his grip on her to pull off his T-shirt. Avalyn took a moment to gape at his defined chest. She forgot Ramsey and his cronies were watching them and traced her finger along his muscular shoulder. Bridger gave her a smile that warmed her much more than the tropical sun.

"You two need a room?" Ramsey asked, laughing to himself.

Bridger rolled his eyes. Avalyn sat down on a rock and unlaced her shoes and slid out of them and her socks. She was not going to take any of her clothes off, even though she had a sports bra on underneath. She'd rather have her blue T-shirt plastered to her chest than nothing covering her as Ramsey's gaze on them never wavered.

She walked carefully into the pool, the irregular stones a little uncomfortable to walk on. Bridger joined her, and as soon as they were waist deep, he dove under. Avalyn bent down and pushed off the rocks but kept her head above water. The pool wasn't huge, but it was deep. They quickly swam over to the waterfall and ducked underneath it. The spray massaged their heads, necks, and shoulders.

Bridger grinned at her. "You're so brave. I worried after yesterday you wouldn't want to be in the water."

She hadn't even thought of yesterday as they swam. "I'm brave when you're with me."

Bridger moved in closer. "I like that," he said.

The water from the waterfall somewhat shielded them from Ramsey and his men. Bridger treaded water with just his legs and wrapped his arms around her waist, pulling her close. The air rushed out of Avalyn. She was falling for him faster than she'd plunged from the airplane this morning. All thoughts of being a strong and independent woman disappeared when Bridger looked at her like that.

"Do you think I might get another kiss of gratitude?" Bridger said, barely loud enough for her to hear over the rush of the water next to them.

"How long can you tread water like that?" Avalyn asked.

Bridger grinned. "A long, long time."

Avalyn knew she should show some restraint or her heart would be a goner. If they ever escaped from Ramsey, she'd shrivel and never be able to love again when Bridger moved on. But in this beautiful setting with the sheet of water next to them, the vines and cliffs on the other side, having just gone through something so horrific as being thrown out of a plane without a chute, and Bridger's strong body close, she really had no resistance in her.

She leaned closer. Bridger's lips brushed hers, and sheer joy encompassed her.

"Hey! Isn't it cool back here?" Ramsey's voice came from much too close by.

Avalyn jerked away from Bridger and glanced over at Ramsey's mischievous smile.

"I'm going to kill you very soon, Ramsey," Bridger muttered.

Ramsey laughed like that was the funniest thing he'd ever heard. "I hope so, my friend."

Bridger shook his head at Avalyn. His arms loosened around her, and she swam through the waterfall and back out. Ignoring all the men around her, she lay on her back and floated, looking up at the blue, blue sky above. She prayed that somehow, someway, they'd get away from this crazy man and she could get back to the children. But then she wouldn't have Bridger holding her close anymore.

When she tired of floating, she swam to the side and the men followed her out of the pool. They both shrugged back into their shirts, and Bridger and Avalyn put their shoes back on.

"Thanks for hanging out with me," Ramsey said, as if they were all friends.

Bridger stared at him. "You have so many screws loose, not even an aerospace engineer could fix that nut-job brain of yours."

Ramsey threw back his head and laughed. "My mom used to tell me I had screws loose all the time."

Bridger looked at Avalyn and did the crazy symbol with his finger by his ear. Avalyn giggled, and then she started laughing and couldn't stop. Bridger and Ramsey both joined in, and Avalyn knew it was insane that she could laugh in the middle of this situation, but it was a release she needed. Then she glanced at Ramsey, who was laughing and looking at her warmly, like she was his younger sister or something. The guy really was insane. At least he hadn't thrown her off the waterfall or sacrificed her to the island spirits.

Avalyn sobered and started back down the trail. She had to get out of this alternate reality, or she was going to be as nuts as Ramsey.

# CHAPTER THIRTEEN

W hen they got back to the yacht, the sun was dipping close to the horizon. Thankfully Ramsey told them good night, so they wouldn't have to endure his presence any longer. The gleam in Ramsey's eyes as he said goodbye robbed the breath from Avalyn's lungs. What would he do to her tomorrow? She couldn't let her mind go there. At least they'd have the reprieve of being together tonight without his weird comments or looks.

Yet as they walked toward their room, her apprehension grew for a different reason. She would've willingly kissed Bridger under the waterfall, but was that smart? How did you ask an adventurer, a free spirit, if he would commit to you and your causes forever, especially in a situation like this? You didn't. It was stupid, and she hated to envision Bridger smirking at her if she did ask. Would he lie and say yes, or would he just laugh and tell her not to worry about tomorrow? She would be with him on that one. She didn't want to think about tomorrow and another chance for Ramsey to kill her.

They entered their room, and Bridger told the guards good night and shut and locked the door behind them. The rolling tray full of food was already waiting for them. Avalyn wondered about Ramsey's staff, especially his guards, who were so devoted to him.

"Hungry?" Bridger asked.

She nodded. They sat down and ate. Avalyn was afraid there would be awkward silence, but Bridger started telling her stories about his brothers when they were younger. He made her laugh quite a few times as she ate some boneless ribs, rice, and broccoli.

After dinner, they took turns showering, and Avalyn waited nervously as Bridger showered. Would he expect to sleep cuddled up again tonight? She'd loved that, but she wasn't sure it was in her heart's best interest. Her nerves were to the stretching point when the bathroom door finally opened.

Bridger strode out in only some low-slung sweats. Avalyn put a hand to her throat, suddenly unable to breathe. Why did he have to look so marvelous? How was she going to resist him? Especially when she'd been the one to ask him to cuddle last night.

He looked her over and said, "You okay?"

Avalyn nodded. She wouldn't tell him that she worried over falling in love with him almost as much as she worried over what Ramsey might have planned tomorrow. Her normal life seemed far away right now, but she worked long days securing funding, speaking or writing about how to help the children and motivate people to be more charitable, and—most importantly—traveling and spending time one on one with her little ones. There were so many adorable faces in her mind. She couldn't simply fall in love and follow Bridger around the world, forget about her purpose in life.

"Thank you for defeating Ramsey again," she said to Bridger rather than beg him to love her and find a way to make their lives coincide.

"I'll do it again tomorrow, unless I find a way to get us out of here first."

Avalyn wanted to trust in his confidence, but she was scared, really scared, of waking up tomorrow.

"It's hard being the best." He gave her a cocky grin.

She rolled her eyes, though she did like his smart-aleck attitude. "I'll bet it is."

Bridger slowly walked toward her. His dark gaze pinned her in place. The muscles in his abdomen and chest rippled beautifully. She wanted to run her fingers along each individual muscle. No! She couldn't let herself go there.

He stopped in front of her and she tilted her head back to meet his eyes, praying for strength and wisdom. She'd asked too much of the good Lord lately, though, and was afraid her prayer quota had been reached. Her mama would tell her there was no such thing, but Avalyn didn't know if even divine intervention could give her the strength to avoid throwing herself at this beautiful man and getting her heart ripped out in the process.

"There's something else I hear I'm the best at," he murmured. His eyes languidly lowered to her lips.

Avalyn's breathing quickened. She could hear waves lapping against the boat and the motor running as she tried to tell herself not to rise to this obvious challenge. "Oh, really? What's that?"

"Kissing."

He gave her his trademark smirk, and all her concerns came rushing horribly back to her. He was a player in every sense of the word. Love 'em and leave 'em was Bridger Hawk's motto in life, right after "What's a challenge, and where do I find it?" That probably applied to women as well. Her mind spun. It did apply to women! He'd said that line to her when he'd kissed her in Cancun the day before Creed and Kiera's wedding. Dang him.

Avalyn's eyes narrowed and she pushed at his chest with her hands.

"What?" Bridger backed up a step, lifting his own hands innocently.

"You hear you're the best?" She folded her arms across her chest. "How many women have you 'heard' it from?"

Bridger arched an eyebrow. "Jealous, are we?"

Avalyn clamped her jaw before she growled at him and revealed exactly how jealous she was. She spun away from him, grabbed a pillow off the bed, and stalked to the couch. Lying down so she faced the couch cushions and the wall, she yanked the throw blanket off and draped it over herself.

For a few seconds, all she could hear was her ragged breathing and the boat's motor. What was Bridger thinking? Did he realize how petty and jealous she was? How she wanted him all to herself? She felt so off in this horrific situation, so unlike her usual confident, benevolent self.

His footsteps slowly approached. Avalyn clenched her fists and refused to look at him. Her heart was racing out of control. Part of her felt justified in her petty jealousies and her refusal to fall for a player; part of her just wanted to kiss him and worship him for rescuing her over and over again.

"Ava?" he said.

Avalyn squeezed her eyes shut.

He let out a frustrated growl, similar to what she'd wanted to express seconds ago. Avalyn smiled in spite of herself. At least she wasn't the only one upset.

Bridger wrapped a hand under her upper back and one under her legs and swept her off the couch.

"Bridger!" Avalyn grabbed on to his shoulders for stability.

He stared down at her, all traces of teasing gone. "You're sleeping in the bed."

"Not with you," she threw back at him.

He stalked to the bed but held on to her. "Fine. I'll sleep on the couch."

Avalyn shook her head. "You can't sleep on the couch. You need to be in prime condition to beat stupid Ramsey tomorrow."

His eyes darkened. Avalyn realized she was still clinging to his shoulders, so she let go and folded her arms across her chest.

"It's a big bed," he said. "I'll sleep on the other side."

"And put some pillows between us."

Bridger rolled his eyes.

"And don't you think about touching me," she said.

"Fine." Bridger kept holding her.

"You're still touching me," she pointed out. It felt much too nice to be held close to his glorious chest like this, the bulging muscles in his biceps pressed against the side of her abdomen and her thigh.

"I won't touch you again," he growled.

"You still are."

Bridger stared down at her and finally pushed out a breath. "You're the most confusing woman I've ever met," he said.

"Why?" She glared at him. "Because I don't beg you to kiss me like all the bimbos who chase you around?"

"You wanted me to kiss you at the waterfall. What changed?"

"I remembered what a pimp daddy you are."

"A pimp daddy?" He chuckled darkly. "You have no idea what I am."

She drew in a breath and refused to answer him.

"You want me, Ava. You just won't admit it to yourself."

Avalyn hugged her arms more tightly to her chest as if she could protect her heart from him. He had no clue how much she wanted him. "You're still touching me," she reminded him tersely.

"It won't happen again." He set her down on the bed and stepped back. "Good night, Ava Baby." The mocking, overconfident Bridger was back, and Avalyn hated it, but at least she knew how to act around him. She could protect her heart from Playboy Bridger. She could remember they had different lives to lead and that the children had to come before her selfish desires to be loved by this man.

Avalyn closed her eyes so she didn't have to look at his beautifully formed body and feel sorry for herself that even though this might be her last night on earth, she'd chosen to not spend it in the arms of the man she loved because of her fears of heartbreak. His footsteps circled the bed, and then she felt the mattress sink as he lay down. She gritted her teeth and hated that tears squeezed past her tightly shut lids.

She should worry that he wouldn't work as hard to protect her tomorrow. Maybe he'd let Ramsey win. But she knew him too well. Bridger was a man of honor, even if he was a player. He would protect her from danger and from Ramsey. If only she could apologize and scoot close. Ask him for a goodnight kiss. Ask him to hold her.

She gritted her teeth and kept her eyes shut, praying she could sleep tonight and somehow survive tomorrow.

# CHAPTER FOURTEEN

B ridger had a hard time sleeping with Avalyn's soft breaths next to him. Her perfect body was close, yet so far away. Why had she picked a fight with him? Why did she think he was some playboy? Well, okay, maybe he liked to play the field, and of course the media made it look worse than it actually was. He wouldn't lie to Avalyn and say he hadn't kissed a lot of women, but why wouldn't she give him the chance to settle down with her?

He woke with a dull headache, and the pounding on the door didn't help at all. The door sprang open before he did much more than sit up in bed.

Ramsey bound in, lit up like it was Christmas morning. "I thought they were lying to me."

"About what?" Bridger growled, standing up to face him. He glanced over to see that Avalyn had also pushed out of bed, still dressed in a T-shirt and some sweats. She looked beautiful with her dark hair tousled and her lips swollen from sleep.

"You two really aren't having any fun at night." Ramsey clucked his tongue, still grinning like the Cheshire cat. "When I win today, I'll show you what it means to spend the night with a real man," he said to Avalyn.

Bridger flew at Ramsey, slamming his fist into his gut. Ramsey doubled over, and Bridger heard guns being cocked as he aimed for Ramsey's still-smiling mouth.

"Stand down, sir," Mike said as four guards rushed into the room.

Bridger stepped back, though he wanted to hit Ramsey repeatedly.

Ramsey straightened, all smiles. "Don't worry, bro. You'll get a chance to fight me soon."

Bridger wondered what that meant. He'd take that chance, anytime. "You aren't going to touch Avalyn."

Ramsey laughed. "We'll see about that." He clapped his hands together. "Get dressed. Clothes like yesterday. We'll eat on the way. Got a few hours' flight each way." He strode out of the room, and the guards filed in behind him.

Bridger looked to Avalyn. She was watching him with that hero worship look she sometimes got, but there was fear in her eyes too.

"Thanks," she murmured. She turned and strode into the bathroom.

Bridger pushed a hand through his hair. Today looked to be the worst day yet. At least on the other days he'd felt like Avalyn wanted to be with him. He should've gotten the memo that she didn't on Christmas Eve in Cancun when he'd kissed her and she rejected him. Then he'd sappily followed her to Long Island, and she'd rejected him yet again. Apparently, he was dense when it came to this woman. He knew she didn't want Ramsey, but it hurt that she didn't want him either.

———

The helicopter ride was excruciatingly long. Avalyn tried to eat some of the breakfast burritos and juices they'd brought with them and look around at the scenery, but it was nothing but ocean for a good portion of the ride. Her rear hurt from sitting, but her heart hurt worse from wanting to be closer to Bridger and knowing she'd messed it all up.

They left the ocean behind and flew over stretches of beaches and lush greenery until they approached a massive black mountain that she was pretty sure was an inactive volcano—at least, there wasn't visible lava. They landed next to the mountain, which looked to be thousands of feet tall, made up of tiny black rocks.

Ramsey had kept up a steady stream of conversation with Bridger, reminiscing about different competitions between the two of them over the years. Bridger talked with him, but his voice was tight, and whenever Avalyn glanced his way, he was looking at her, not Ramsey.

Avalyn tried to hide her worry over what the contest might be today and her longing for Bridger. The combination gave her a huge headache, and the ride in the chopper didn't help anything.

They all exited the chopper and Ramsey gestured around at the mountain covered in tiny black rock. "I rented out the volcano for the day."

There was no one around but them, but there was a stack of weird wooden sled-like things close by.

"Everybody grab one." Ramsey picked a sled up and gestured for them to follow.

Avalyn picked one up also. It wasn't terribly heavy. Maybe today they wouldn't just throw her down the volcano without anything but Bridger to save her.

"I'm glad you like to hike," Ramsey said. "Let's go." He started up the hill. Bridger and Avalyn fell into step next to him. It was a decent hike and the sun was already hot, even though it couldn't have been much past ten a.m.

They hiked quietly, the sound of the volcanic rock sliding under their shoes their only accompaniment. Avalyn's throat was dry and her legs burned. The incline continued on and on. When they finally reached the top, they were all dripping sweat. Avalyn glanced at the flatter top surface that sloped down into a crater. They weren't close to it, but she was still afraid Ramsey would shove her down the hole.

"Today won't be near as bad as the other days," Ramsey said to Avalyn.

"So you're not going to try to kill me today?" She planted her hands on her hips and glared at him.

He chuckled. "I hope not. I really want my chance to stay with you." He winked.

Bridger growled low in his throat, "Ramsey." It was a warning that would terrify most men.

Ramsey simply laughed. "Man, I like you two. But I sense some tension today. I take it the kiss under the waterfall wasn't as romantic as you'd hoped?"

Avalyn felt heat flush her face. She glanced down the mountain. "So what's the challenge?" The anticipation was torture, and she just wanted it to be over.

"Ooh, so quick to change the subject." Ramsey whistled. "Sorry, brother. I guess she's gunning for me to win today."

Avalyn spun to glare at him. "You stay away from me."

Ramsey roared with laughter. "We'll see, sweetheart. We'll see." He pointed down the slope. "Have you done this before Bridge?"

Bridger shook his head.

"Not a lot of skill to it, but it's dangerous and fun. They usually wear protective gear, but we don't care about that. More dangerous the better, right?"

Avalyn rolled her eyes at him, wishing she could slug him again, but she felt the least fear she'd had since this crazy competition had started. She'd ridden plenty of sleds down snowy slopes. This was steep, but even if they went faster than she'd ever gone on a snow sled, it was nothing compared to being drowned or thrown from an airplane. The chances of survival were infinitely higher, especially if she had her own sled.

"Now you sit or lie on the sled," Ramsey continued, pointing back down the slope they'd climbed up. "The lower you get your body, the faster you'll go. If you want to slow down, just put your feet down—but not too hard, or you'll flip yourself, and this volcanic rock can leave a mark." He pointed to a scar on his chin.

Avalyn waited for the punch line. "That's it? I just have to ride this sled down the volcano? You're not going to drown me or sacrifice me in the volcano?"

"Not today, sweetheart." He winked, then gestured. "You go first. We'll be catching you soon."

Avalyn glanced at Bridger. He gripped the sled tightly, staring at her. There was something in his eyes she didn't like. This wasn't his usual event, and Ramsey had done it before. Would this be the day Ramsey won? She couldn't let herself think that. At the moment, she was simply relieved this didn't seem as bad as the past two days.

The helicopter hovered in the air a short distance away with a cameraman standing in the open doorway. She sat on the sled and looked at the camera. "What's a challenge, and where do I find it?" she said jauntily.

The other men laughed, and Bridger cracked a smile at her. "You got this," he said.

Avalyn nodded to him, then pushed off, sitting up. The sled gained momentum quickly, and it would've been a fun ride if she wasn't worried about Ramsey catching her or tipping the sled and ripping her face and arms apart. She glanced over her shoulder and could see the men were coming now. They were both lying down and angled right at her.

Avalyn wondered if she could steer to the left so Bridger could reach her more easily, but then she wondered if she shouldn't lay down herself and try to go faster and have neither of them catch her. She'd demand Bridger get his own bedroom, and she could sleep in peace tonight.

She lay back and the sled sped up, but as she looked back, the men were still gaining on her and there was a lot of mountain left. She needed to try to steer the thing to the left. As frustrated as she and Bridger were with each other, she couldn't risk Ramsey winning this challenge.

She could hear the whoosh of their sleds coming closer and closer as she sat up and tried to pull at the handles to guide her to the left. It didn't work. Shoot. She put her feet out and pushed her right foot in, thinking she could shove herself to the left. The sled veered to the right instead, like she'd dug a rudder in.

She glanced back and saw Ramsey shove Bridger's sled to the left with his foot. Avalyn cried out and tried to pull on the handles to avoid him. Ramsey grinned, angling closer. He was almost upon her. Bridger was too far to the left. He would never reach her first. No, oh no!

Ramsey was only a few feet away. She prayed and tried to turn the stupid sled somehow. Going to the right would take her farther from Bridger; turning to the left would let Ramsey run right into her. She couldn't escape. Ramsey edged nearer, nearly touching her sled now.

"Bridger!" she yelled.

"Ava!" Bridger was closing in on them, but he'd never reach them in time.

Ramsey leapt from his sled and landed right behind her on her sled. He spread his arms wide and stood behind her like he was surfing. "Yes!" he hollered. "Yes!"

Avalyn's heart slammed against her chest. "No," she whimpered.

Ramsey sat down behind her as the sled whooshed down the hill. "Isn't this fun?" he asked.

Avalyn didn't answer. Her heart was thudding against her rib cage and her grip was so slick she could hardly hold on to the handles.

They coasted down the last of the incline as it leveled out. Ramsey jumped up and extended his hand to her. Avalyn ignored his outstretched fingers and stood on her own. Her legs were shaky, but there was no way she was relying on Ramsey. Fear clawed at her throat and her stomach turned over and over again. Even being pushed out of an airplane wasn't as terrifying as the thought of fighting him off all night long. If she even could.

Bridger's sled came to a rest and he stood. Avalyn looked at him. His proud shoulders were bent forward and a look of misery clouded his handsome face. He said nothing, and that scared her as much as anything, as if he were resigned to her fate.

"I finally won!" Ramsey punched a fist in the air and jumped around a few times. "You guys ready for lunch?" he asked as if Avalyn's world wasn't crashing down around her.

Ramsey led the way to a covered picnic area. There was a large lunch spread on the table, sandwiches, salads, sushi rolls, veggie and fruit platters. The entire group was somber, except for Ramsey. He didn't rub anything in, which surprised her, but he just had this perma-grin on his face as he ate and chatted with one of the guards about a heli-skiing competition in Switzerland that he and Bridger had competed in last year. Bridger had won, but that didn't bother Ramsey. Nothing seemed to bother this guy.

Bridger ate methodically, not looking at any of them, even her. Avalyn couldn't stomach food right now. She pushed some around on her plate and drained a couple of water bottles, but that just made her stomach more squeamish. If only Bridger would glance at her, somehow reassure her that it would all be okay. But they both knew the truth. It wasn't going to be okay.

———

Bridger felt the pain of his failure rounding his shoulders, weighing him down like no burden he'd ever experienced. The unthinkable had happened. He hadn't won. Avalyn would be subject to that monster Ramsey tonight. How could he have failed her? He wanted to yell out his anguish and pound at his chest. Instead he ate slowly, forcing food in as his mind scrambled for an option, any option.

They finished lunch and Ramsey said happily, "Let's go, boys." He gestured toward the helicopter.

Bridger was having an out-of-body experience as they trudged back to the chopper. He wanted to grab Avalyn and shield her with his body as Ramsey's men pumped him full of bullets, but what would that accomplish? Then Avalyn would be subject to Ramsey every night instead of just tonight. Pain lodged in his chest. Ramsey touching Avalyn. It was too horrific to allow his mind to go there.

Avalyn was going to hate Bridger even more for failing her. Why had he fought with her last night and this morning instead of holding her close and begging her to not think about the other women he had kissed, to concentrate on how much he loved her and only her?

He stewed through the chopper ride, but no brilliant ideas to protect Avalyn hit him. They arrived back at the yacht in the late afternoon. How was he going to survive when Ramsey took Avalyn to his room? He cast a guilty look at her. Her eyes were closed and she'd wrapped her arms around her abdomen like she was praying. He should pray too, but there wasn't much hope or faith left in him. He'd tried so hard, and he'd failed her.

They walked down the steps from the chopper, stopping on the rear balcony. Ramsey spread his hands wide. For once, his perma-grin was nowhere in sight. "This is where we part ways."

Bridger knew he couldn't fight them all, but he had to try something. He stepped up to Ramsey and said, "Please don't do this."

Ramsey's blue eyes glinted at him. "Why not? I've earned my night with her."

Bridger swallowed, but the lump in his throat stayed firmly in place. "Ramsey. We've competed for years. We respect each other. We've been friends a long time."

Ramsey nodded in acknowledgment.

"Please," Bridger repeated. "You can't do this. I'll do anything you want. Lose any competition to you. Shout all over the media how great you are." He was desperately trying to think of anything that might convince Ramsey not to touch Avalyn. Money meant nothing to him, only fame and women. Women. Not Ava. Not the woman he loved. *Please Lord, help us.*

Ramsey silently smirked at him.

"Please," Bridger tried again. He glanced at Avalyn. She was the picture of beautiful innocence with her dark hair trailing across her shoulder and her dark eyes staring at him with such tenderness and fear. He couldn't let Ramsey hurt her. He lowered his voice and admitted to Ramsey, "I love her."

Ramsey's blue eyes lightened. "That makes it even better."

Bridger let out a growl and lunged at Ramsey. A taser hit him in the back, and a shock of pain surged through him.

"Bridger!" Avalyn yelled.

His face slammed into the slick floor. He jerked and grunted in pain as his body writhed from the electricity. The taser finally released its agonizing grip on him, but immediately arms grabbed him from behind. The four men each took an arm and a leg. Gripping him tightly, they hauled him through the main area, down the hall, and into the suite he and Avalyn had shared. He could hear Avalyn screaming for him until they were out of earshot. They tossed him on the bed, and one of them secured his hands behind him with some kind of strap.

Then they walked out, the door closed, and he was left horribly alone. His body slowly stopped quivering in pain, and

Bridger slid to the edge of the bed and off. The pain had receded, but he felt exhausted and drained. He couldn't let that stop him, though. He had to protect Avalyn.

He ran and threw himself at the door. It quivered but didn't budge. He backed up and rammed it again, leading with his shoulder. The door held and he heard grunts on the other side. The guards had to be pushing their weight against it, holding it closed. Why didn't they just let him bust through and shoot or tase him again?

"How long do you think he'll fight?" he heard one of the guards ask.

"How long would you fight if it was your girl?"

"All night."

Bridger nodded. At least they knew he wouldn't give up. If he stopped, it would be conceding the love of his life to Ramsey. Anger and hatred coursed through him. Today, somehow, some-way, he was going to rip Ramsey apart.

"Avalyn!" he screamed, slamming his body against the door again.

# CHAPTER FIFTEEN

valyn followed Ramsey to his suite, climbing up a set of stairs above the main living room of the yacht. She felt detached and cold, so cold. She noticed details that didn't matter. That his suite was bigger than hers. That the idiot never stopped smiling. Would the guards come into the room with them, or would she have a fighting chance with Ramsey alone? She knew he was strong, but this was her virtue she was fighting for.

"Thanks, guys." Ramsey nodded to the guards, then shut the door and turned the lock. The lock turning was like a death knell to her heart. "Why don't you go shower?" Ramsey asked, pointing toward an open door.

Avalyn didn't want to do anything he said, but at least in the bathroom she'd be away from him. It was prolonging the inevitable, but at this point she'd take any reprieve she could get.

She hurried into the bathroom, shut and locked the door, and dropped her dirty clothes on the floor. The shower was a huge granite enclosure. She let the warm water pound at her scalp for a while. What was she going to do? How was she going to escape? Her stomach rolled with apprehension and terror, but for some reason, her thoughts kept turning back to Bridger. Had he really begged Ramsey and said, "I love her"? Was that just his ploy to get her away from Ramsey? It hadn't sounded or felt like a ploy. Tears mingled with the shower water. She loved Bridger, and there was little hope of her getting away from the psychotic Ramsey.

She thought she heard the bathroom door open. She gasped and backed into the corner of the shower.

"I set out some clean towels and clothes for you," Ramsey called.

"Get out!" Avalyn yelled.

His only response was a deep chuckle and the bathroom door closing a moment later.

Avalyn's heart thumped uncontrollably. Ramsey forcing himself on her seemed worse than free-falling without a parachute.

She shut the water off and carefully stepped around the shower wall. Ramsey was gone, and there were a couple of towels on the counter, next to a silky floral dress. Her clothes were nowhere in sight. So it was go face him in only a towel or put his stupid dress on. Avalyn let out a frustrated and terrified yelp and then forced herself to dry off, brush out her tangled hair, and slip into the dress. There was perfume and makeup on the counter also, but she ignored them.

The dress was flattering with a V-neck and no sleeves. It came a few inches above her knees. She hated what Ramsey had dehumanized her to—a pretty face and a hot body. That wasn't her. She hated him worse than any media person who'd made fun of her causes or politician who tried to block her efforts. She'd never loathed a person like she loathed him.

Avalyn took a deep breath. She wondered what Ramsey would do if she stayed in here all night. She eyed the small window. Could she squirm out through it? She'd rather take her chances with the sharks than with Ramsey.

The door swung open and Ramsey stood there. His dark hair was wet, and he was wearing a button-down white shirt and khaki pants. Had he showered in another suite? Could she have escaped while he was gone? Despair and frustration traced through her.

He gestured out of the bathroom. "Let's eat."

Avalyn drew in a breath, squared her shoulders, and stalked out to face him. No matter what, she would show how strong she was. She was Avalyn Shaman. He could take advantage of her body, but he would never kill her spirit.

A similar rolling cart like the one that came into her and Bridger's room was stacked with trays. Ramsey didn't say much as he offered her food and ate himself, but his grin never disappeared. The awful tension made her jumpy, and her stomach twisted so badly that she could only eat a little bit of each dish. She prayed in her mind desperately for help and protection, but the heavens seemed as silent as this room.

"Did you get enough to eat?" he asked, looking pointedly at her still-full plate.

"Yes," she muttered.

Ramsey stood. He eased closer to her like a jaguar stalking his prey. Reaching down, he grabbed one of her hands before she could pull it away and tugged her to her feet. His smooth palms felt like a snake against her bare skin. He looked her over carefully.

"Now." His voice lowered. "I have to know the answer to one question before we proceed."

Avalyn could hardly breathe, let alone talk. "What?" she spat out, tilting her chin as if she were royalty. Her mind spun with which self-defense moves she should lead with. She doubted she could beat him, but she would try to hurt him like he was going to hurt her.

"Our boy loves you."

Avalyn had been touched deeply when Bridger had said that, but she didn't know if it was a ploy to soften Ramsey or if it could really be true. Could Bridger Hawk truly love her and settle down to one woman? Why was she worrying about that when she was facing Ramsey?

"The question is—do you love him too?"

Avalyn's eyes widened. She studied Ramsey. Why would he care? He was going to take advantage of her regardless. There was no reason to lie, though. She tilted her chin up and said, "Yes, I do."

Ramsey chuckled, bobbing his head several times. "That's beautiful. It's just beautiful."

Avalyn's stomach swirled with nausea. Ramsey thought it was beautiful because he was going to hurt her so he could beat Bridger. He was so sick and twisted. She would fight to her last breath; that she knew for certain. He could possess her body but never her mind.

He released her hand and gestured toward the door. "Go."

Avalyn backed up a step, eyeing him. She felt like a deer in a hunter's spotlight, unsure which direction to run and ready to be gunned down at any minute. Was he being serious? A flutter of hope rose in her chest, but she didn't dare trust it and especially didn't dare trust Ramsey. Everything had been a twisted game since he'd kidnapped her.

"You're an impressive woman, Avalyn Shaman. I love your bravado and your charitable heart. I think you're one of the most beautiful women I've ever seen."

Avalyn's heart was racing out of control. She didn't need or want Ramsey's compliments, and she was terrified they meant he was going to enjoy hurting her.

That twisted smile grew on his face. He looked her over, then chuckled. The sound scraped over her like the edge of a knife being dragged along her skin. "But I would never want to touch the woman who was truly in love with Bridger Hawk." He winked at her.

Avalyn's breath rushed out. She still wasn't certain what kind of ploy this could be. Ramsey wouldn't allow Bridger to win, let her escape, would he?

Ramsey walked to the door and pulled it open. Two guards were standing there. "Please escort Miss Shaman back to her suite."

The guards nodded and stepped back. Avalyn looked to Ramsey, waiting for the trick.

He simply smiled at her and said, "Enjoy your night with my friend. I think you'll like tomorrow's challenge. You aren't even involved."

She blinked at him. This evil man had just preserved her virtue and told her she could go to Bridger. She didn't wait to be told again. "Thank you," she whispered. She hurried past him and the guards and out into the hallway, then down the stairs. Her speed picked up as she reached the main area.

"Bridger!" she yelled. Relief rushed through her, and the anticipation of being in his arms made her legs weak. She pressed on toward the hallway where her and Bridger's suite was. Ramsey had let her go. Soon she'd be in Bridger's arms. She hadn't felt such joy since she'd been kidnapped three days ago.

"Bridger," she called out again.

She heard the guards running behind her chuckle. She smiled too, not caring if they were laughing at her or with her. Bridger was all that mattered now.

# CHAPTER SIXTEEN

Bridger slammed into the door more times than he could count. His shoulder was throbbing and he was making no progress. He slid to the floor, despondent and nauseous. For a very long time, the only sounds he heard were his ragged breathing and his painfully thumping heartbeat.

Avalyn. What was she enduring at Ramsey's hands while he sat here in this rejected stupor? How could he give up on saving her? He drew in a steadying breath and said a lengthy prayer for Avalyn's protection and help from above. With effort, he stood and spoke to the guards through the door. "Guys, please. What if it was your girlfriend or wife?"

The silence on the other side was deafening. What had Ramsey done to gain such allegiance from his men? Bridger had liked the man before this nightmare, but now he thought he was a psychotic sadist. Money couldn't buy the loyalty Ramsey had with these men. Yet there had to be something, some way for Bridger to break through their shields.

He slammed his head against the door, then hung it, shame and despair fighting within him. How could he fail Avalyn like this? "Please." It came out as a croaked whisper. He cleared his throat and tried again so they could hear him. "Please help her. Think if it was your wife, your girlfriend, your sister, your niece."

Bridger pressed closer to the door, praying inside. He needed so much help, and he didn't know where to find it. Creed would've already taken the entire group of mercenaries out and swept the love of his life into his arms. Bridger cursed himself for not choosing a military career. Why had he wasted so much time being the best at untraditional sports? It was superfluous and idiotic. Who cared about fame or excitement if he couldn't protect Avalyn?

He heard nothing on the other side of the door. He slammed it with his body again and then collapsed against it. Tears traced down his face. He didn't know the last time he'd cried, probably when he was little and his brothers were teasing or torturing him. He'd gotten pretty tough with three older brothers. There was nothing tough about him right now. He was weak and his life was meaningless.

He faintly heard his name being called. He straightened. Was he delusional? It sounded like Avalyn. Pressing closer to the door, he listened again. There it was. Avalyn was yelling his name.

"No!" he hollered, not able to stand thinking about what Ramsey must be doing to her. She was calling out for Bridger, and he could hear it this far away. There couldn't be a worse torture in the world.

"Avalyn! Ava!" He backed up and ran at the door again. He rammed against it, and the door popped open.

The guards stood back, grinning at him. Mike held out a

knife. Bridger's eyes widened and his stomach dropped. "For your hands," Mike explained.

"Thank you." Bridger turned, and Mike cut his hands free. "Thank you!" he yelled again, taking off at a run down the hallway.

Avalyn was running right at him. Bridger's steps faltered. She was free?

"Bridger!" she screamed. She slammed into him.

Bridger lifted her off her feet and swung her around. "Avalyn!"

Guards surrounded them and Bridger tensed, sheltering her with his body. They weren't taking her from him again. He didn't care if they killed him. He couldn't go through the past hour again. He'd rather die.

"Sir," one of the guards said. "Why don't you go into your suite? I'm sure you'd like some privacy." He winked.

Bridger stared at him, hardly able to comprehend what he was saying. He glanced down at Avalyn's beautiful, shining face. "Ramsey let me go!" she said, beaming.

Bridger shook his head in disbelief.

"It's true." Avalyn laughed, looking young and fresh and beautiful. Was it really possible? Her innocence and light had been preserved?

Bridger looked to Klein, who nodded. "He asked us to escort her back here," Klein said.

"Thank you," Bridger managed to croak through the lump in his throat. He felt weak all over again, but for very different reasons this time. He swooped Avalyn off the floor, held her against his chest, and strode down the hallway. She smiled up at him, so happy and absolutely radiant. Avalyn was okay. She was in his arms. Nothing else mattered.

Bridger pushed through the door and closed it behind him. He walked to the couch and sank down with her still in his arms. Burying his head in her soft hair, he let out a choking sob. "Ava." He simply held her close for a few seconds and she burrowed into him, clinging to his neck. "He didn't ...?" He finally dredged up the words, but he couldn't finish the question. She didn't appear to be harmed, but he had to be sure.

"No."

"No?" Bridger raised his head and studied her deep brown eyes.

She shook her head, and a shudder raced through her body. "I thought he would. He told me to shower and left me only this dress to put on."

Bridger took in the dress. It was beautiful on her, but the thought of Ramsey making her wear it for him, of reducing Avalyn to little more than her exquisite face and body ... He swallowed down the bile rising in his throat.

"I was praying for strength to fight him off, but then ..." She studied him for a few beats and then looked away. "He just told me to go."

Bridger wondered if there was more to it than she was telling him. There was something in her eyes, and he didn't like that pause. He focused on the one beautiful truth, that Ramsey hadn't taken advantage of her. "Maybe I won't kill him when I see him again," he muttered darkly.

Avalyn blinked at him. "He said that I'd like tomorrow's challenge, that I wasn't involved."

Bridger processed this. "Maybe he's starting to feel guilty for putting you through all of this."

She shrugged.

"Today's challenge was awful because I didn't get to you, but it wasn't as dangerous as the last two days. I was sure you almost drowning that first day really shook him up. Maybe he's going to alter the challenges to just involve him and me, for his publicity stunt to keep going, but not risk you anymore."

Avalyn simply stared at him.

"What are you thinking?" he asked.

"I'm thinking I don't want to think about him anymore."

Bridger pursed his lips. "Today took about ten years off my life."

She shifted on his lap, pressing closer to his chest, and ran one hand from his neck up into his hair. Warmth rushed through him. "I'm sorry you went through that." She leaned in and kissed the side of his mouth.

Bridger groaned and wrapped his hands tighter around her waist. "Ava," he whispered.

She smiled slightly. "Maybe I could make it all better if you'd just shut up and kiss me."

———

Avalyn bit at the side of her lower lip as Bridger's chest rose and fell quickly. Had she been too bold? He'd told Ramsey he loved her earlier. Did he mean it, or was he just trying to protect her?

"Now that sounds like a beautiful plan." Bridger grinned, then lowered his head to hers. Their lips connected, and happiness soared within her. He manipulated her mouth carefully, tenderly. There was nothing demanding or insistent about the kiss. It was as if he thought she was a priceless treasure.

He pulled back and framed her face with his hands. "Ava," he whispered. "I was so afraid."

"Me too," she admitted.

"I won't let him near you again." His deep brown eyes studied her with sincerity.

Avalyn didn't know how Bridger could promise such a thing with all the men Ramsey had, the guns they constantly flaunted, and the awful taser they'd hit Bridger with today. She knew he was sincere and after tonight she hoped Ramsey wouldn't do that to them again. Maybe Ramsey didn't want her anymore. He claimed he'd let her go because she admitted she loved Bridger. Should she tell Bridger that?

Bridger didn't wait for her response; he bent his head to hers and claimed her lips like he'd been waiting for this chance his entire life. This kiss was firm and strong, and Avalyn loved it as much as his tender kisses. Bridger's warm hands moved confidently against the silky material of her dress. She was hot from head to toe, but she also felt such love and possessiveness. Bridger was sworn to protect and love her. The combination of sweet and fierce was overwhelming and beautiful to her.

The kisses heated with passion and swelled to a crescendo. Avalyn never wanted to come back down to reality. Bridger slowed the kisses down and held her close. His lips lingered next to hers. Their breath intermingled, and she savored the closeness.

"I love you, Ava. I've loved you since I was twelve," he murmured against her lips.

Avalyn straightened and stared at his beautiful face. If that was true, what did love mean to him? She loved Bridger, but sadly she still didn't trust him to be able to devote himself to her and only her once they returned to the real world. That was what she'd always dreamed of with Bridger, and he'd never delivered before. She couldn't delude herself into believing he would change just because of the situation they were in.

"You're joking," she said.

"Why would I joke about that?" His hands still held her tight to his body as if he couldn't stand to let her go.

Avalyn didn't want to have this talk. She wanted to savor her escape from Ramsey, kiss Bridger all night long, and bask in Bridger saying he loved her. But she'd loved him as long as he'd claimed to love her, and he had repeatedly chosen to flit from girl to girl and break her heart. "You've tormented me since we were teenagers, and the one time you kissed me, you went and made out with Kelly Turner in front of the entire school the next day." She'd been a senior and thought finally she and Bridger were going to have a chance, but he'd proven her wrong quickly.

Bridger's brow furrowed. "You have to understand that you were two years older than me and perfect in my eyes. I kissed Kelly to make you jealous so you wouldn't dump me. I know it was stupid now."

Avalyn pushed off his lap and stood. She needed some distance from him and his excuses.

Bridger stood also. He looked fierce and strong. She would never be afraid of him physically, but he'd hurt her so many times emotionally as she'd longed for him from afar all these years and watched through social media as he flitted from woman to woman.

She suddenly regretted the intense kissing session they'd just had. Yes, she was relieved Ramsey hadn't taken advantage of her, and she was touched by Bridger's apparent devotion, but she knew better than to trust that he'd settle down to one woman. Hadn't he proven that with Britney on Christmas Eve?

Avalyn was so out of sorts right now. She didn't feel like a philanthropist, author, and speaker, but like a needy woman who only existed for this one man. "So all the women you've had clinging to you throughout the years were just to 'make me jealous'?"

His brow furrowed.

"Being all over Britney Nolan at Creed's wedding? That was just to make me jealous?"

He lifted his hands and shoulders. "In my defense, that was—"

"Last week," she supplied, folding her arms across her chest.

"Stupid. I was going to say stupid." He took a step closer, his broad frame overshadowing her. "Plus the fact I kissed you the day before and you shut me down with no hope of you being interested."

"I only shut you down because you're such a player."

"Those other women meant nothing to me, Avalyn." He brushed her hair back over her bare shoulder, and her skin tingled in response. "It's always been you for me. Always."

Avalyn wished she could believe him. "Well, those other women meant a heck of a lot to me."

"They did?" His eyes narrowed.

"Yeah. I've loved you every bit as long as you've loved me, and those other women have gouged my heart out. They meant the man I loved was a player who would never settle down to one woman. Never settle down to me."

Bridger caught her in his arms. He pulled her against his chest, and Avalyn couldn't resist him. "I was wrong," he said. "I should never have dated or kissed anyone but you. I didn't know you loved me. I thought you were out of my league and I'd never be worthy of you."

"Honestly?" She pulled free of his embrace and took a step back. "That's the stupidest excuse you've had yet. You're

Bridger Hawk. You haven't lacked for confidence a day in your life."

"Is it?" He arched an eyebrow. "I've always thought you were the most exquisitely beautiful and perfect woman in the world— my dream woman. You told me yourself that our paths are different, basically that I'm a selfish thrill-seeker and you're a charitable philanthropist."

She had said that, kind of. It sounded awful as he threw it back at her. "I'm sorry, Bridger. I didn't mean it like that. My life isn't glorious or glamorous like people think. Most of the time I'm sleeping on a cot, living on rice, and working long hours to make a child's life better. We just have different paths. We've each chosen our lifestyles, and I don't know how they'd ever coincide."

"Our paths have been different, but that doesn't mean we can't love and complement each other's careers and vision. You think I just jet-set around the country from party to party, but that's not true either. At every event I'm trying to help the children too, and a lot of times we're camping out to be in the right place for a certain challenge. It's not extravagant or glamorous."

Avalyn pulled in a breath. She'd never thought of complementing each other's dreams, mostly because she'd never thought Bridger could truly love her—before these past few days. It wasn't really about living conditions and money, though. She still wondered if he could love her like she wanted to be loved. He was famous and handsome and woman weren't going to stop fawning over him and seeking his attention. What if she devoted herself to him and he fell back into his old patterns? Could a player like him ever be faithful to one woman?

He studied her. "If I'd come to you at any point in our adult lives and told you what you meant to me, how deeply I love you ... would you have believed me?"

Avalyn's breath caught. She loved him, but was it enough? "Probably not," she admitted.

"What do I have to do to get you to trust me?"

Several beats passed, and the room felt stifling. Finally, Avalyn admitted, "I don't know, Bridge."

He sucked in a breath.

"Our lifestyles are just so different. We're so different."

Bridger didn't try to touch her. His gaze was hollow and sad.

"Let's just get through this nightmare with Ramsey. It's silly to worry about us as a couple when we may never escape this boat." Ramsey could kill or rape her tomorrow. Who knew?

Bridger stared down at her, then said in a rough whisper, "We don't know what tomorrow will bring, but I do know I love you, Avalyn. I don't have all the answers for us, but I just ..." He pushed a hand through his hair. "Can I keep you close tonight?"

A tremor passed through her at his words and his tender request. Tonight might be their last night on earth. She didn't want to spend it fighting with him or theorizing why they wouldn't work, especially after the horror of being captive in Ramsey's room, fearing the monster would take advantage of her.

She walked over to the bed and pulled the covers down. "You're right," she admitted.

Bridger walked slowly toward her, a smoldering look in his eyes that robbed her of her breath. He slipped out of his shoes and slid into the bed, reaching up for her. Avalyn couldn't resist him any longer tonight; she lay down and cuddled close to his side.

She wished they could kiss the night away, but she'd have to content herself with being in his arms. She couldn't afford to let her desire for him take control and deal with the regrets that would surely come. If they got back to the real world, would she feel his arms around her again or have to watch him with other women? She closed her eyes shut, inhaling his musky scent and pushing those fears away.

# CHAPTER SEVENTEEN

Avalyn felt groggy when she woke the next morning. She slowly blinked open her eyes and realized she was still cuddled into Bridger's side, her cheek pressed into his muscular shoulder. She glanced up at his face. His eyes were closed, so she could simply study him. She loved the defined planes of his face, the strong jaw shadowed with dark hair, the regal nose and brow, and those intriguing lips that were the perfect fit for hers. His dark lashes rested against his upper cheek, but she could easily picture how they framed his eyes so perfectly.

She loved him. Not just because he was beautifully formed, but because of his fun, confident personality and his love and zest for life. Seeing this serious, protective side of him the past few days had only made her love him more.

His eyes slowly blinked open and he stared at her. His trademark smirk tilted his lips and he said, "You enjoying staring at perfection?"

"Oh, you!" Avalyn pushed at him, but she laughed. "Always with the overconfidence."

"It's one of the many things you love about me."

"Yes, it is," she admitted.

Bridger's cocky smile disappeared. "Is it really?"

Avalyn gave him a quick nod, then wiggled out of his arms and stood quickly. She was still in the silky dress from last night, and it felt ridiculous in the light of day. She didn't know where she and Bridger stood, and she realized it was in her court to decide. Maybe today would be the day this awful competition ended. Maybe, when they got back to the real world, she and Bridger could find a way to make a relationship work with their very different lives. If he reverted to his old style and countless women in his arms, she'd have to learn to deal with her broken heart. Somehow.

"I'm going to shower and get dressed," she said.

He nodded, still studying her much too seriously.

Avalyn rushed into the bathroom, where her suitcase was, and hurried to shower, not bothering to wash her hair. She got dressed in a comfortable pair of shorts and a T-shirt. Her stomach tumbled as she thought of kissing and loving Bridger, but she forced those thoughts away and wondered what today would bring. Ramsey. How would he act after last night? She felt indebted to him for letting her go, letting her return to Bridger. Yet this nightmare was all Ramsey's creation, so she didn't want to feel any gratitude to the man.

Breakfast was waiting when she exited the bathroom. She waited while Bridger showered and dressed. When he walked out looking fresh and irresistible in a blue tank top and gray shorts, she sharply sucked in air. How could she resist this man?

Her eyes traveled over his handsome face and down to his

chest and arms. She gasped and rushed toward him. "What happened to your shoulder?" His right shoulder was black and blue.

Bridger glanced down at his shoulder and grinned. "I rammed it into the door a few ... hundred times." He pointed at the door, which looked more battered than his shoulder. "Sadly, the door won."

Avalyn half laughed and half cried. He'd bruised himself trying to get to her. She wrapped her hand around his forearm, then bent down and pressed her lips to his shoulder. Bridger groaned, and heat filled her belly.

He cupped her chin and tilted her face up. "You missed the spot. My lips are up here." He grinned, but there was nothing cocky about it. This grin was downright sexy and meant for only her.

Avalyn laughed for real this time. "I guess I'm not a very accurate markswoman. Can you help me out?"

"Gladly." He cupped her cheek with one hand and wrapped his other hand around her lower back to pull her flush against him.

Avalyn melted against his broad chest, and when their lips connected, she trembled under his touch. His lips maneuvered hers in a pattern that was becoming familiar, but it was still so exciting she could hardly stand on her own two feet. Luckily, she didn't need to stand with his strong arms supporting her.

There was a rap at the door. The lock turned and it swung open to reveal Mike. "Oh, sorry to interrupt." He pushed a hand over his bald head. "Chopper's ready to go."

Bridger smiled down at Avalyn. "I'm sorry he interrupted too."

Mike chuckled, and Avalyn winked at Bridger. Bridger

released her, and they both filled plates with food and cups with juice. Mike said, "You eat quick. The chopper will wait."

Bridger arched an eyebrow at Avalyn as Mike stepped back out of the door but left it open so they could come when they were ready. "You'd think we were honored guests or something."

She sank into a chair and speared a bite of eggs. "Or something. I'm so ready to be done with this crazy train." She smiled. "Or crazy boat and helicopter ride, I guess I should say."

He nodded, but his eyes grew serious. "I worry when we're done you're going to slip away from me again."

Avalyn's bite of eggs caught in her throat. She coughed and then took a long drink of apple juice. She couldn't promise anything at this point. Bridger's actions when and if they ever escaped Ramsey would determine their future.

They ate the rest of their breakfast in silence, then took turns brushing their teeth before they followed Mike to the helicopter.

Ramsey's grin was so broad as they settled into the helicopter that Avalyn didn't know what to think. Should she be afraid of what he was planning, or hope that maybe he was their friend now?

"You two have a good night?" he asked.

Bridger grunted in response. Avalyn squirmed. She'd loved sleeping in Bridger's arms, but the tension between them was growing worse as her fears and indecisiveness lay between them. Part of her wanted to throw her worries out the helicopter door and simply love Bridger until the day she left this earth, which sadly might be today. No matter what Ramsey said about her not being involved today, she didn't trust him after he'd almost drowned her on day one, thrown her out of this very helicopter without a chute, then terrified her last night that he would take advantage of her.

Yet she couldn't commit to Bridger when they were in this delusional reality. She wondered what it would take for her to commit to him, to believe he wouldn't ditch her for another model as soon as those options were available again. Bridger Hawk just wasn't the type of man to settle down and live in the suburbs—but then again, neither was she. Could their dreams come together?

"We've got a shorter flight today. Settle in and enjoy the scenery." Ramsey winked and then took his own advice, leaning back and staring out the window.

Bridger and Avalyn strapped on their seat belts, and the chopper took off. They flew over the ocean but soon were over land. It was the Caribbean, so the island was lush and green. They flew over a sprawling city, and Avalyn wondered if it was Belize City. It looked a lot like it.

They landed at a small, overgrown airstrip. A few Hummers were waiting for them, and some of the guards from the boat were already there. Had they come earlier in the chopper or taken the speedboat in? They all piled into the vehicles. Nobody said much as they drove through city streets.

They stopped behind a large warehouse-looking building. The guards slid the doors back, and everyone walked inside. Avalyn's eyes adjusted to the dimly lit open room. There were sets of temporary silver bleachers situated around a boxing ring. She glanced at Bridger. He looked at her and shrugged.

Ramsey strolled in front of them down to the ring. He turned and spread his arms wide. "Today could be our last challenge, my friends, and you'll say goodbye to me forever."

Avalyn's stomach leapt with apprehension of what this challenge might be, hope that this would really end, and dismay that she might no longer be with Bridger every day and every night.

Ramsey grinned. "You've been wanting a chance to beat the life out of me, right, Bridge?"

Bridger shrugged and then smiled. "You know me well."

"Yes, I do." Ramsey laughed low and deep. The sound was eerie and foreboding. Avalyn didn't know him well, but she didn't like the little she knew. Even though he'd set her free last night, he'd used her as a pawn and almost killed her.

"So here's our last challenge," Ramsey added. "Bridger and I fight. No gloves, no protective headgear, no rules, no referees."

Avalyn's stomach churned more and more. What awful trick did Ramsey have up his sleeve? She looked closely at his hands, searching for brass knuckles or something shady like that. Her eyes then went to his ever-present bodyguards. Did they have a taser or worse to zap Bridger with if he truly thumped Ramsey? She didn't doubt Bridger could win, but she doubted it would be a fair match.

"What happens when I pummel you?" Bridger asked.

Avalyn focused in on him. He stood there so brave and strong, like a fierce warrior who would never bow to the adversary. She loved his spunk and strength and especially his protectiveness of her. Yet she remembered one of his YouTube videos. He and Ramsey had sparred, and it had been awful to watch. They'd gone at it until they were both bloody, but the fight had eventually been declared a draw. How long and how hard would they fight today? She hated that it would be an even match. What if Ramsey won?

Ramsey laughed. "If you knock me out, you both go free and you'll never see me again."

Avalyn's heart leapt. Going free and never seeing Ramsey again sounded wonderful.

"I like the thought of knocking you out and being free," said Bridger, as if reading her thoughts. "How can you promise I'll never see your ugly mug again? Maybe I'll come with my own hired thugs and take you out."

Ramsey grinned. "I'm all-powerful. You should know that, Bridge." His smile left. "I can promise we'll never see each other again ... after you knock me out."

Bridger studied him. Avalyn was interested in Ramsey's terminology but couldn't make much sense of it. She wouldn't mind if Bridger did hire his own bodyguards to come track Ramsey down after what he'd put them through. Better yet, he could work with Creed and his Navy SEAL buddies, kick Ramsey's butt, and then turn him in to the proper authorities. She was sure there was nothing Ramsey would hate worse than rotting in a jail cell. He should have to feel what she'd felt these past few days—fear, uncertainty, misery, and despair.

"Let's do it." Ramsey pulled his shirt off and dropped it on the floor before heaving himself up onto the ledge of the ring and slipping through the ropes. He stretched his arms behind his back, making his chest muscles pop. He was fit; there was no doubt about that.

Bridger turned to her. "A kiss for good luck?" he asked.

Avalyn's mouth dropped open. "How can you think of kissing at a time like—"

Bridger pulled her in close and cut her off with his lips. She melted against him and returned his kiss, joy radiating through her from his touch and supple lips.

He released her and winked. "I can think of kissing you at any time."

Avalyn pressed a hand to her lips, ignoring Ramsey's laughter from the ring. "Come on, Bridge, don't rub it in that you won the girl."

Bridger lifted his shirt up and over his head and dropped it on a nearby bleacher. Avalyn's mouth went dry as she studied the defined muscles of his chest, shoulders, biceps, and abdomen. The bruising on his shoulder reaffirmed that he'd go to any extreme to protect her. She framed his face, lifted onto tiptoes, and kissed him again.

She whispered against his lips. "A kiss for good luck, not that you need it."

"I always need your kiss." He smiled.

"Kick his trash," Avalyn said.

Bridger chuckled. "You sound like my sister-in-law Cambree now."

Avalyn smiled. Bridger turned and strode to the ring, jumping onto the side using only his legs, like a weight lifter doing a box jump, and then sliding through. He looked strong, confident, and irresistible.

The men strode toward each other and bumped both fists. Ramsey was grinning, as usual. "It's been a great ride, my friend. Thank you."

Bridger inclined his chin. "Not ready to thank you yet."

Ramsey roared with laughter at that. "You will soon."

Bridger shook his head. "Nut job."

They backed away and started circling each other.

Mike gestured to the bleachers. "Would you like to sit?" he asked Avalyn.

She shook her head. "I don't think I could."

He nodded and stayed standing next to her. Oddly enough, Avalyn had grown to like some of these bodyguards. Besides the fact they upheld Ramsey's wishes, were paid mercenaries, and had tasered Bridger last night, they seemed like good guys.

She focused on the men in the ring, who were slowly moving toward each other. Bridger was strong, but Ramsey would most likely do something underhanded. It was his typical mode of operation.

Ramsey led with a solid swing to Bridger's abdomen. Bridger grunted, but the hit hadn't fazed him at all, and he moved in close and his fists started swinging. He hit Ramsey with repeated punches, the muscles in his broad back flexing with each punch. Ramsey got in his fair share of hits. Avalyn cringed each time, sometimes crying out, especially when Ramsey slammed his fist into Bridger's bruised shoulder. After one vicious roundhouse to his shoulder, Bridger fell back, his face contorted with pain.

Avalyn wanted to go to him, hold him. Instead, she stayed rooted to her spot, praying and wringing her hands together. If Bridger won, they would be free and maybe they could figure out their relationship. If he lost ... who knew what Ramsey's next challenge would be?

———

Bridger had been aching for this fight for the past four days. He came out swinging, and Ramsey didn't disappoint, trading hit for hit with him. It felt great to slam his fists into Ramsey's body and let out his frustration and anger over his former friend putting him and Avalyn through these insane challenges.

They pummeled each other for who knew how long, and though the hits hurt, especially the ones to his sore shoulder, he didn't slow down. Last time they'd fought, neither of them had won, but today he had to win this battle. He would. It was past time to get Avalyn away from this monster and prove that he would love her and only her.

Ramsey popped him in the nose, and in the resulting burst of pain, Bridger heard the crunch and felt blood gush out. "I had to give you something to remember me by," Ramsey said.

Bridger wiped it away with his hand and moved back in. "You keep thinking you'll escape once you set me free." He slugged him hard in the abdomen, and Ramsey grunted. "Have you heard of Sutton Smith and Creed Hawk? We'll come for you and you'll be rotting in a prison cell before the end of the week."

Ramsey laughed and jabbed him in the shoulder again. "That looks sore, Bridge."

Bridger hit him with an uppercut to the chin. Ramsey's head flew back, but he simply danced around and grinned. Bridger wiped the blood off of his nose again with the back of his hand.

"You're ticked at me, right, bro?" Ramsey taunted.

"You have no idea," Bridger said, slamming his fist into Ramsey's side. The man had endangered and terrified the woman Bridger loved desperately. Ticked didn't begin to describe the way he felt toward Ramsey right now.

Ramsey pointed at the side of his head. "Then take me out!" he yelled. "I'll give you a free shot. You deserve it after these past few days."

Bridger eyed Ramsey, waiting for the trick. He might break his hand on Ramsey's skull, but that point on the side of Ramsey's head—right below his ear—would definitely knock the guy out. It would be worth a broken hand to end this and be done.

"Come on!" Ramsey hollered at him, turning his head to give him an easier shot.

A primeval yell ripped out of Bridger's throat as he took the shot. He smashed his fist into Ramsey's head. Ramsey went down hard. His head whiplashed as he hit the mat, bounced, and then settled.

Bridger wanted to dive on him and keep hitting, but he forced himself to unclench his fists. Ramsey's eyes were shut, but Bridger could see his chest rising and falling. He heard footsteps and looked over to see Ramsey's men infiltrating the arena. Bridger put up his hands and stepped back. "He told me to take the shot."

"We know, sir," Klein said. He gestured out of the ring as other men dropped to their knees next to Ramsey.

Bridger was amazed once again at their devotion. He shrugged it off and strode to the edge of the ring, slid out, and then jumped to the ground. One of the men handed him a wet towel and a water bottle. He used the towel to mop up his face, gingerly touching his nose, which was probably broken. At least the bleeding had slowed.

He focused in on Avalyn. She stared at him for half a beat; then she ran and threw herself into his arms. Bridger pulled her in tight with his free arm. He was sweaty and bloody, but she didn't seem to care. He held her close, loving her in his embrace.

Avalyn glanced up at him. "You did it. We're finally free."

He smiled down at her, but his stomach felt sick. He'd just knocked Ramsey out, but Ramsey had let him, had told him to hit him in the head. Why? He glanced back up at the ring. Men were still surrounding Ramsey.

"I hate to interrupt," Mike said at Bridger's elbow, "but our instructions are to get you two back to Miss Shaman's plane and send you on your way. Her pilot and stewardess have been informed and are awaiting your arrival."

"What about Ramsey?" Bridger couldn't believe he cared, but

Ramsey had yet to stir. Why had Ramsey given him a fair fight? Why did he taunt Bridger to hit him in the head and end it all? What did that mean? What if Bridger had hit him hard enough to cause brain damage or something?

"They'll take good care of him, sir." Mike ushered them toward the door.

Bridger kept one arm around Avalyn, clutching the bloody towel and water bottle with his other hand. He glanced back as they exited the door. He could only see Ramsey's feet and a cluster of men bent around him. Ramsey still wasn't moving.

# CHAPTER EIGHTEEN

Mike got them settled in the back of a Hummer and handed Bridger an iPad. "He requested that you see this after you won, sir."

Bridger met Mike's gaze. "What's going on Mike?" Nothing in his racing mind could explain the turn of events today.

"It's all working out like it's supposed to." Mike tapped on a video displaying Ramsey's smiling face and then shut the door.

Avalyn took the iPad from Bridger, and he smiled his gratitude as he drank from the water bottle, then wiped at his face with the damp towel some more. He must look like a total mess. He'd forgotten to grab his shirt, and his sweaty back stuck to the seat. But all he cared about was that Avalyn was safe and they were done. A feeling of relief washed over him. He said a silent prayer of thanks that they'd survived and Avalyn's virtue had been preserved.

Avalyn pushed the play button as Mike climbed in and started the vehicle. The video spun for a second, then started playing. Bridger hardly noticed the vehicle pulling out onto the quiet street. His gaze was fixed on the image of Ramsey, standing on the deck of his yacht, grinning like he always did.

"Bridger, my friend. I wanted to say thank you and you're welcome." Ramsey eyes twinkled. "The thank you is for making my last days memorable." He paused.

"Last days?" Bridger questioned Mike.

"Please just watch, sir," Mike said.

Avalyn pressed into Bridger's side and stared up at him. He tried to smile reassuringly.

"I have a brain tumor," Ramsey explained. "It's wrapped around my brain stem and growing rapidly."

Avalyn gasped. Bridger felt dizzy. He sucked down another gulp of water, his eyes riveted to his former friend.

"I found out last week when I passed out surfing. The doctors all told me surgery was impossible, and as aggressive as the tumor is, it would put pressure on the brain stem and I would be dead very soon." He shrugged his shoulders. "Not great news, so I decided to go out with a bang." With a wink, he said, "I apologize for any stress on you or Miss Shaman. I am prepared to keep her safe, even though you have no way of knowing that. If you're watching this, it means you've won and hopefully you've hit me hard enough to speed my miserable end. The research shows a hard hit to my head will end it all."

Bridger's heart hammered against his chest. Ramsey had used Bridger to kill himself? He hated Ramsey even more right now, but at the same time he felt sorry for him. The guy was certifiably crazy, but Bridger couldn't imagine knowing you were going to die. What would he do? How would he act?

He felt Avalyn against his side. He wouldn't have risked anybody else's life; that was for sure. He'd never forgive Ramsey for that. Even though the man thought he had safety precautions in place, they'd come close to losing Avalyn in the water and in the air.

"So I thank you for being with me at the end and for ending it for me. I've always thought of you as a close friend, Bridge. I respect you and bow to your superiority. You always win, but I'm okay with that now." Ramsey grinned again. "The reason I say you're welcome is because of me bringing Avalyn Shaman into this."

Avalyn pulled in a breath. Bridger wrapped his arm around her and hoped his touch was comforting. He probably stunk to high heaven.

"You think your love for her is so secret, but I knew about it years ago. Remember? We were doing a surf competition in Australia, and there was a live feed of Avalyn helping some village on the news. You were glued to it, and when I asked you about her, you said, 'My dream woman, so out of my league it's laughable.'"

Bridger grimaced as the memory resurfaced. It was still true.

"I watched you over the years, and no matter how many women you were with, I could see you only wanted her."

Avalyn stiffened against him. Bridger wanted to correct the way Ramsey had phrased that, but the video was continuing.

"So I set this all up for a fun competition, to spend my last days with my favorite opponent, a man I respect above all others, and to hopefully push your dream woman into your arms. I hope you get the love I know you deserve. You're the best, man." He gave a thumbs-up.

"Avalyn," Ramsey continued, "I apologize for what I'm going to put you through the next few days. I may die at any time, and then you'd avoid some of the challenges. It'll be fun to see. I hope you give my friend Bridger the love he deserves, and I hope someday you won't hate me as much as you probably do right now. You can tell your kids about their crazy Uncle Ramsey who brought you two together." He wrinkled his nose. "A guy can hope, right?"

Bridger hoped she would love him also; the thought of kids made his heart swell. He wanted children, with Avalyn. He knew and understood her reservations. He would work through them, no matter how long it took.

"As you may know, I haven't been able to burn through my close-to-a-billion-dollar inheritance yet." He chuckled. "Dang money keeps making me more money. Each of my bodyguards has received ten million dollars and will disappear after the last challenge so they receive no repercussions for their part in this little idea of mine. They are my best friends, next to Bridger, of course. The rest of my money—I believe it's four hundred million and change—I've donated to Health for All, your company."

Avalyn leaned heavily into Bridger, putting her hand to her mouth.

"I know you have no problem fundraising with friends such as the Hawk Brothers, but I wanted to do my part." He grinned and spread his hands wide. "Go save the world, pretty lady— with Bridger by your side, of course." He saluted the screen. "See you in the next life, friends."

The film stopped, freezing on his broad grin. Bridger's emotions were all over the place. He hated Ramsey, yet he felt for him and they had been friends a long time.

The vehicle was silent, and Bridger played back his memories of the past four twisted days. His mind went beyond that, and he remembered all the times he and Ramsey had competed, joked, and pushed and challenged each other. It was insane, but he'd miss Ramsey.

Mike was navigating into the airport drop-off zone. Bridger caught his eye in the mirror as he stopped the Hummer. "What happens now?"

"You both fly home," Mike said. "Miss Shaman's pilot has the plane ready to go."

Bridger was grateful for that, but he had to know. "And Ramsey?"

"They'll take good care of him. They're taking him to a private island that he loved. As soon as he passes, they'll bury him there." Mike offered a grim smile, then pushed his door open and stepped out to get their door.

Bridger slid out and helped Avalyn. Luckily, his nose had stopped bleeding, and he figured he had wiped off most of the blood. He looked at Avalyn. "Think FAA is going to let me into the airport?"

She wiped at his cheek. "You're kind of a mess."

Mike met them on the sidewalk with Avalyn's suitcase and Bridger's bag. He handed them each a passport.

"Where'd you get these?" Bridger asked.

Mike laughed. "You should know by now Ramsey is all-powerful."

Bridger laughed too. He stuck out his hand.

Mike gave him a firm shake, then backed away. He nodded to Avalyn. "It's been a pleasure getting to know both of you."

"Where are you going to go?" Bridger asked.

Mike smiled, rubbing at his bald head. "I've been hankering to open a little sandwich and ice cream shop somewhere in the Caribbean. Maybe I'll find me a local beauty to help me."

Bridger nodded. "Put lots of sunscreen on that head."

"Yes, sir." Mike smiled, tipped his head to them, then strode around to the driver's side. He slid in, and within seconds he was gone.

Avalyn wrapped her arms around herself. "Ramsey was completely insane, wasn't he?"

Bridger nodded. He felt a strange letdown that it was over. Competing with Ramsey over the years had been challenging and exhilarating. Now that his friend was gone, what would he do? He glanced down at Avalyn. His first order of business was to convince her that he'd be there for her.

He zipped open his bag, found a T-shirt, and shrugged it on. Straightening, he grabbed Avalyn's suitcase and his bag. "Ready to go home, Ava Baby?"

"I thought you'd never ask."

Bridger had a lot more questions for her, but he'd save them until they were safely in her plane and he'd showered. He needed to smell and look his best if he was going to talk her into his future plans.

# CHAPTER NINETEEN

Avalyn reclined into the leather seat. What a relief to be on her own plane and flying toward Long Island. She wanted to hug her family members for a long time.

The sound of water running in the bathroom reached her ears. She longed to hug Bridger again. What was going to happen between them now that they weren't thrust together in this insane challenge?

Bridger came out of the bathroom a few minutes later, looking handsome in a gray Henley and deep blue chinos. His dark hair was wet and his face was clean of blood. She winced when she noticed his nose looked a little bent.

Avalyn gestured to the chair next to her. It would be much better to have this conversation without him pulling her close. She needed to remain levelheaded. Somehow. As his musky scent washed over her, she knew levelheaded was a lot to ask of herself.

"You look ... nice," she said.

Bridger grinned. "I'm like ranch."

"What?"

"Dressing done right—smooth and creamy."

She laughed, loving that he could always find a way to tease. He definitely was smooth. "You and your overconfidence."

He winked, sat, and angled his body toward her. "You doing all right?"

Avalyn's heart squeezed. How like him to be concerned about her. "I'm tired and emotional and angry and grateful." She nodded to him. "Confused."

Bridger took her right hand between both of his. "You don't have to be confused about me, love. Just know I'm never leaving your side, and it makes it easy."

Avalyn's throat went dry, and warmth surged through her. What she wouldn't give to agree with him. He should definitely never leave her side. Yet how could she figure things out with him nearby? His smell alone confused her thought processes. "Bridge ..."

He bent his head closer. "I don't like the sound of that 'Bridge.'"

Avalyn pushed out a shaky laugh. "I think we need some time ... and space, to figure out where we stand."

Bridger's mouth pursed. "I know where I stand—right next to you."

Avalyn put a hand to her heart. "You're killing me here."

The corners of his lips lifted into a cocky smirk. He lifted her hand and kissed the back of it. Avalyn trembled from his simple touch and the desire and dedication in his eyes. "After I've worked so hard to protect you?" he asked.

Avalyn smiled. "Thank you, Bridger. These past few days ..." She shuddered. "The only good part was you."

He studied her for a few beats. "Yet you still don't trust me," he said quietly.

Avalyn pulled her hand free, and she rested her hands in her lap. "I know you're a good man, one of the best, but your lifestyle ..." She shrugged. "I guess you're right. I don't trust that you won't just fall back into old patterns with women as soon as we hit the ground and they flock to you as usual."

"I can't even see another woman when you're around, Ava."

She clutched her hands. "Can you please give me some time to see that for myself? To believe that you're done being a player?" Ramsey's testimony that Bridger had always loved her had touched her, but Ramsey had said in the next breath something about all the women Bridger had been with. She hated that.

Bridger's brow furrowed. "How much time?"

"I don't know. Let's just deal with all the media that Ramsey probably created with this mess and go back to our lives. I'll know when I can trust you."

"So I'll stay with you always. Then you can see that I couldn't care less about other women." He nodded as if it was all decided.

How Avalyn wished she could agree. The thought of being apart from him hurt deep down. "I've watched you through the media for a long time, Bridge. I think that's the best way for me to watch and decide—from afar."

"The media always skew things. You can't trust those idiots."

"They can't skew your arms around a woman."

He shrugged and blew out a breath. "So you're going to go back to your life and I'm going to go back to mine, and then, what, in a week we'll get together?"

"Not a week." Even a week sounded too long, but she had to do this, had to know if he could be faithful to her. "Maybe a month."

He clenched his fist and bounced it against his leg. "I hate this, Ava. I just want to be with you."

"Maybe for the first time in your life you'll have to wait for something, prove you really want it."

His eyes narrowed. "That was hurtful."

Avalyn laughed. "Really? You know I'm telling the truth. You're naturally talented, handsome, and insanely wealthy. Everything you've wanted falls right into your lap."

"Everything but you." His gaze intensified.

"I guess you really do owe Ramsey for that," she said flippantly.

Bridger undid her seat belt, wrapped his hands around her waist, and plucked her right out of her seat. Avalyn gasped as he transferred her quickly to his lap. "I'll give you your month, if that's what you want," he said, his breath short and his gaze never leaving her face. "But I want you to know exactly what you're missing out on every minute we're apart."

Avalyn had no strength to protest as his lips covered hers. The kiss was intense and full of passion and love. Bridger's desire and commitment came through the kiss. She'd never felt so needed and wanted. His hands stayed safely around her waist, but his kiss promised a lifetime of passion, caring, and happiness … if she'd only say yes.

Avalyn pulled back, her chest heaving and her heart thumping out of control.

"I love you, Ava," Bridger said. "I'll give you all the time and space you need, but you have to know there's no one for me but you. I'll never give up on us."

Avalyn's eyes stung with tears and her throat tightened at his tender words. She wanted to throw her stupid month to the wind, but she had to be sure he would be true to her. She had to.

She'd worked too hard to create, maintain, and implement her charity to throw it all away on a dream of a man who might not stay by her side. At the moment, though, she simply wanted Bridger. She cuddled into him, resting her head on his shoulder. "I hope you don't," she murmured.

Bridger kissed her forehead, then simply held her close. Avalyn savored their connection even more than normal. A month apart was going to be more miserable than being in Ramsey's power.

# CHAPTER TWENTY

Avalyn fell asleep in his arms. Bridger had no desire for sleep, only for her. He cradled her against his chest and prayed hard. Prayers of gratitude for them both being safe. Prayers of forgiveness for Ramsey and his stupid, crazy challenge and him making Bridger hit him hard enough to probably kill him. Mostly prayers for Avalyn's heart to soften and trust him. It sickened him that he'd hurt her so many times throughout the years. He'd kissed many other women to try to forget about her. He'd had no clue his actions were the reason he couldn't be with her. Hopefully over the next month he could prove to her that she was the one for him.

A month without her? He rubbed his hands along the curve of her waist. How was he going to survive?

The plane started its descent, and Avalyn stirred. She glanced up at him, her beautiful face irresistibly close. Bridger couldn't resist one more tender kiss. Avalyn moaned and kissed him back. His heart raced.

A throat cleared. "Please buckle in for the landing," the flight attendant said, laughter in her voice.

Avalyn pulled away from him, climbed into her own seat, and smoothed down her hair. "Thank you, Ivy."

The woman nodded and exited the cabin through the back door.

Bridger extended his hand. Avalyn secured her seat belt, then rested her palm against his. Bridger wrapped his fingers around her hand. "You sure about this month idea?"

Avalyn didn't smile. She nodded quickly. "At least a month, Bridge."

He squeezed her hand. "You'll be calling me to come to you within a week."

Avalyn did laugh then. "Always with the overconfidence." She squeezed his hand back. "Thank you for giving me time."

He nodded. "I'm going to hate it, but I'd do anything you asked, Ava." He hoped she hated their time apart as much as he knew he would.

"I know you will, Bridge."

The plane touched down, and Bridger wished they didn't have to face the real world. They exited the plane and were ushered through the airport. As soon as they cleared the security gates, their families and reporters rushed around them. Bridger clung to Avalyn's hand, but they were separated as they hugged family and reporters tried to elbow their way in.

Bridger's mom was sobbing, and he held her close until she calmed down. "First Creed gets captured, dies, and comes back from the dead, and then you have to do these insane challenges. You boys will be the death of me."

"I'm sorry, Mama."

"It's not your fault, love."

Plainclothes FBI agents pushed their way in and took Bridger and Avalyn to a back hallway in the airport. Bridger watched as Avalyn was escorted toward a room. She raised her hand and said, "See you in a month."

His chest tightened. He made a heart with his hands. "You'll be calling me sooner."

Avalyn simply smiled, and then she was gone.

The agents ushered him into a different room; luckily, they allowed Creed to come in also. Bridger told them everything that had happened the past four days, and they explained that Ramsey started releasing the videos yesterday morning, so they'd seen Avalyn's near drowning and her being thrown from the helicopter. They'd been scrambling to trace Ramsey and his yacht. This morning, they'd gotten a notice from Ramsey's attorneys that Avalyn and Bridger would be flying into the airport between two and four p.m. After confirmation from Avalyn's pilot, Creed had taken a flight back.

The other agents and several of Sutton Smith's men were trying to track down Ramsey and his men, while others were interviewing his accountants and lawyers, who all claimed innocence.

Bridger smiled. "I'm sure they are innocent, or Ramsey would've given them an escape hatch like he did his men."

Creed arched an eyebrow. "Such as?"

"Ten million each, and they're all disappearing. I wouldn't waste time going after them."

"You wouldn't?" one of the FBI guys asked.

Bridger thought of Mike and Klein. "You can, but you'll waste a lot of time and resources on guys who were just following orders."

"You're sure Ramsey's dead?" Creed asked. "This could all be a ploy so we don't search for him either."

"Could be." Bridger shrugged. "But to what end? He's never been on the FBI's radar before this week. Why would he do all of this if he wasn't dying?" He folded his arms across his chest. "I'm sure he went to the best brain surgeons in the world before he gave up. Research that avenue and you might have some answers."

They all nodded.

The questions and philosophizing continued. Bridger answered, but his mind was in the next room, with Avalyn. Was she really going to ditch him for a month? That sounded harder to survive than Ramsey's crazy challenges.

# CHAPTER TWENTY-ONE

Avalyn was at a one-room clinic on the island of Cape Verde, Africa, helping administer immunizations to children. She didn't have medical training, but it wasn't really necessary to fill out paperwork, put Band-Aids on, and give the children hugs and lollipops. Her nurses were very competent.

She'd stayed busy the past few weeks and only let herself think about Bridger and how much she missed him late at night as she lounged in a cot by herself. Sleeping in his arms had been heaven. Often she remembered Ramsey's words about Bridger saying she was out of his league. That was ridiculous; Bridger was everything she'd ever wanted.

When she'd finished with the questioning with the FBI, she'd gone home with her family. Bridger had honored her wishes and hadn't contacted her. That had surprised her and hurt, which was silly, because he was honoring her wishes. She'd traveled to four continents and eight different countries the past few weeks, visiting and working with the children and arranging for the huge increases in funding with her clinics around the world, getting teams in place to start expansion with Ramsey's money. As he'd promised, over four hundred million dollars showed up as an anonymous donation.

"Would you look at that?" Callie, a bubbly blonde nurse, whistled. "I guess only you can imagine Bridger Hawk smiling at you like that."

Avalyn's eyes darted to the television screen. Sure enough, there was her dream man. He was grinning at the morning talk show host, and they were highlighting the new program he'd started to host extreme sports competitions and donate all the proceeds to the anti-trafficking battle. She'd read about this last week, and she was proud of him. It was a fitting cause, considering what they'd gone through being captured. It seemed he'd found his purpose without her.

She'd scoured the internet as she lay in her cot by herself at night, but she hadn't found any new pictures of him with any women. Only lots of stories about his new competitions and how charitably minded he was. Of course it had only been three weeks. Surely the women would break through into his arms soon. Would he really find her in one more week? He'd said he'd give her a month. She wasn't sure she wanted it any longer. She simply wanted him.

She looked at his smile on the TV screen. Yes, she could imagine it. She'd been the blessed recipient of it many times, yet never enough. And now she'd pushed him away. Why she'd thought a month was a good idea when she was coming off of a highly emotional and horrifying experience was beyond her.

"Yeah, she can imagine it," a deep male voice said behind her.

Avalyn whirled and dropped the Band-Aid and the lollipop in

her hands. Bridger stood there in all his irresistible beauty, grinning at her from the doorway of the clinic.

"She's the only one I want to smile for," Bridger continued. He strode slowly toward them, his smile turning into a smoldering look that gave Avalyn heart palpitations.

"Oh my, I think I'm going to pass out and he's not even looking at me," Callie muttered.

Avalyn smiled, but it disappeared as Bridger drew closer. She stood and backed into the counter. He kept coming. When he was less than a foot away, he stopped and his eyes slowly traveled over her. "I've missed you, Ava Baby," he murmured.

Avalyn swallowed and managed to squeak out, "What are you doing here?"

"Let's go outside and give them a minute," she heard Callie say to the children and the other nurses. Bless her. Avalyn wanted much more than a minute alone with Bridger.

Bridger lifted his hand and tenderly traced it along her jaw. "The thing is, I listened to what you said."

She arched an eyebrow, her jaw tingling from his warm fingers. "You did?"

"Yeah. You had some valid points about me needing to prove that I was fully committed to you. But the part about us being apart for a month?" He pulled a face. "Yeah, that part was stupid."

"It was?" She grabbed on to the countertop behind her for support. She agreed with him entirely: the decision had been stupid, and all she wanted was him.

"Very. I made it through three weeks, and I've never been so miserable. So the new plan is, I prove to you that I'm fully committed while I follow you around the world and help you with your causes."

"Bridge," she whispered.

"Can I follow you around, Ava?"

She couldn't say no to him. She bobbed her chin. "We could try it."

He suddenly dropped to one knee and pulled something out of his pocket. "If we're going to be together, I can think of a way that will be a lot more fun."

Avalyn put a hand to her heart, but she couldn't stop it from racing out of control.

Bridger flipped the box open, revealing an exquisite diamond solitaire set in a gold band. "I love you, Avalyn Shaman. I've loved you my entire life. Will you marry me and let me follow you around the world?"

Avalyn pulled in and pushed out several breaths. She was so in love with him, but she was still scared. "What if you stop loving me?" she whispered.

Bridger stood quickly and wrapped his left arm around her back. "Not possible. I could never stop loving the woman who's exceeded my every dream." He tugged her away from the counter and against his chest. Holding up the ring box, he whispered, "Please, Ava. Give me a chance. I swear to you on my mama's honor that you're the only woman I have ever loved and will ever love."

Bridger adored his mama. He wouldn't do anything on her honor unless he meant it.

She stared into his deep brown eyes and whispered, "Yes."

Bridger whooped. He took her left hand and slid the ring onto her finger; then he dropped the box on the counter and lifted her off her feet, swinging her around and whooping again. Avalyn put her head back and laughed. Bridger slowly lowered her to her feet and gave her the smirk that used to infuriate her.

Avalyn framed his face with her hands. "Just for the record, I've loved you longer than you loved me."

He shook his head. "Not possible."

"I'm two years older than you. I know it's true."

"You just have to have something to argue with me about, don't you?"

Avalyn bit at her lower lip. "Why don't you kiss me so I'll stop?"

"Now that is the best idea you've ever had."

Avalyn gasped in protest, but he cut it off with his lips. She melted into his arms, her legs turning to liquid heat. She loved this man, and she couldn't wait to spend every minute with him and let him prove that he'd never leave her side.

Bridger lifted her tighter. She was snug against his chest and had no plans of leaving his arms again as his lips took control of hers. His lips eradicated every other thought. They would travel the world together, and who knew when they'd settle down in the suburbs next to her parents? But that didn't matter. Bridger was the only home she needed, and being in his arms was the haven she'd been searching for.

# EPILOGUE

Avalyn had always dreamed of a traditional church wedding. As she sauntered down the aisle with a gauzy veil covering her face on her dad's arm, she knew today was going to be perfect.

Bridger stood up front with all of his brothers, looking so handsome in his tailored tux he took her breath away. That slight smirk on his lips robbed the oxygen from her lungs.

"Impressive men," her dad murmured.

They were indeed. From Creed the Navy SEAL to Callum the billionaire tycoon and Emmett the Texas Titans receiver— they were all impressive. But nobody was as impressive to her as Bridger. Her mom was afraid Bridger would demand they ride a wheelie on his motorcycle into the church, but *her* Bridger wanted this day to be whatever Avalyn wanted. He loved her completely, but still would make her life a crazy and fun adventure. He stood tall and strong and his smirk changed to a grin.

That secretive, wonderful grin that Bridger reserved only for her.

They finally reached the front of the chapel and her dad put her hand in Bridger's. Her white gloves made it so she couldn't feel his palm like she wanted, and her veil didn't necessarily obscure her vision but it made him a little blurry.

Her dad responded to the preacher about who gave this woman away and said the traditional, "Her mother and I do." He tenderly lifted her veil and kissed her cheek before letting the veil drop and backing away.

Avalyn turned with Bridger to face the preacher. The ceremony started and she felt happy and perfectly at peace next to the man of her dreams with all of their friends and family here for their special day.

"Excuse me for a second," Bridger interrupted the preacher's monologue about the sanctity of marriage.

Avalyn turned to her future husband, not sure what he was up to, and also not surprised he was up to something. He took one of her hands in his and tugged the glove off, handing it over to Kiera, who stood closest to them on the bridesmaids' side. Then he repeated the action with the other glove.

He wrapped both of his hands around hers and said, "Much better."

Avalyn and a lot of the crowd laughed. The preacher started talking again and Avalyn agreed—Bridger holding both of her hands in his, sans gloves, was much better.

"Excuse me again, Pastor," Bridger said.

The man actually sighed and the crowd tittered with laughter.

Avalyn bit at her lip but couldn't help laughing. "What now?"

Bridger turned her to face him and lifted the veil away from her face and back over her hair. His eyes swept over her face. "Much better," he said again.

Avalyn laughed. Her traditional wedding plan wasn't really up Bridger's ally, and that was just fine with her.

"Can we proceed now?" the preacher asked.

Bridger cocked his head to the side and studied her, giving her a sly wink. "In a minute," he muttered to the preacher.

Then he wrapped his arms around her waist, pulled her flush against him, and kissed her as thoroughly and deeply as she'd ever been kissed.

Avalyn dropped her bouquet, wrapped her arms around his neck, and returned the kiss wholeheartedly.

When Bridger finally slowed the kisses down she registered the crowd laughing and cheering, the preacher muttering something under his breath, and Creed saying, "Did you expect anything less with Bridger?"

Avalyn laughed and moved in to kiss him again. Bridger grinned against her lips and then he was kissing her and her traditional wedding and the disgruntled preacher would have to wait. This was their day and nothing about their life would be traditional so why should their wedding be?

The kiss continued with joy, tenderness, passion, and a promise that Bridger would love and honor her always. No words or vows exchanged could say it as beautifully as his lips did.

---

## Hawk Brothers Romance
*The Determined Groom*

*The Stealth Warrior*
*Her Billionaire Boss Fake Fiance*
*Risking it All*

# HER BILLIONAIRE BOSS FAKE FIANCE

Slipping on a patch of black ice, Lexi cried out, wind-milled her arms, and skidded over the asphalt. She prayed she wouldn't fall. The low thrum of an engine rolled over her as a single headlight flashed across her vision. Lexi screamed, horrified to see a motorcycle flying right at her. She was still skidding on the ice, trying to stay upright. If she fell, the motorcycle would run her over without even seeing her until it was too late. She shuffled on the ice, trying desperately to get out of the way and hoping her waving arms might warn the driver.

The cyclist must've seen her and clenched the brakes hard, because she heard a yell and saw the huge bike lift onto its front tire. Then the motorcycle hit the patch of ice, and Lexi launched herself out of the way as it skidded onto its side. Her feet slid out from under her and she hit the ice with her knees and hands. Pain spiked up her arms and thighs. She felt a rush of wind, and then—miraculously—the motorcycle skidded past her, metal screeching against ice and asphalt. The machine slid to a stop at the curb twenty feet away, minus its rider, who lay sprawled on the cold asphalt, not far from Lexi.

"No, no, no!" Lexi cried out. She crawled across the patch of ice, praying the person wasn't dead and praying no other vehicles came along and finished them both off.

She reached the man, who was dressed in a navy-blue suit that even a girl from Montana could guess was worth thousands of dollars. The suit was tailored perfectly for his large frame. Thankfully he wore a helmet, and she couldn't see any blood or bones poking out. Lexi shuddered. He was lying on his side, facing away from her.

"Oh no! Please don't be dead!" She glanced up at the heavens and called, "Please, Lord, don't let him die." There was no time for folding arms and decorum when a man's life was hanging in the balance.

The man in question groaned and rolled over onto his back.

"Sir?" Lexi touched his shoulder with her gloved hand, breathing a sigh of relief. At least she wasn't responsible for his death. "Sir, are you okay?"

"Not dead yet," he muttered. He undid his chin strap and pulled off his helmet.

Lexi gasped. Staring up at her was a handsome face she'd recognize anywhere: deep brown eyes, dark hair, tanned skin, and short facial hair that only enhanced his good looks. One of the famous Hawk brothers. America's Most Eligible Bachelor. The most handsome man in existence. Her new boss.

"Callum Hawk," she breathed out.

He arched an eyebrow at her and pushed to a seated position, then stood. At least he didn't move like he was broken. He tucked his helmet under his left arm and offered his right hand to her. "We should probably get out of the street in case any other crazies are awake this early." He flashed her the trademark smile that had women across America needing blood pressure medication.

Lexi took his gloved hand and let him pull her up. She was glad they were both wearing gloves, because the surge of energy that went through her simply being this close to him wasn't smart to experience with anybody's boss, let alone a new employer who didn't even know who she was. She'd just made Callum Hawk crash his motorcycle. Jiminy Christmas, she was in trouble!

He released her hand, wrapped his arm around her lower back, and guided her out of the street toward his motorcycle as if they were on a summer stroll through Central Park. Her heart raced out of control. Callum Hawk had his hand on her sweaty back and she'd wrecked his motorcycle. This was not good. She was going to get fired before she even set foot in his office. How would she help her family if she got fired?

"Are you damaged?" Her words came out too breathy and too high-pitched, as her throat was closing off. The motorcycle accident was her fault, but when she died of heart failure from his tingly touch, it would be all on him. "Shouldn't we call 911?"

Callum glanced down at her, his dark eyes filled with concern. "Do you need medical attention?"

"No." She pushed the word out, shocked that his first worry was for her. "But I just made you crash your bike, skid across the asphalt, and most likely ruin that beautiful Armani suit."

He chuckled, stopping next to his tipped-over motorcycle. "It's Brioni."

Lexi's eyes widened and she swayed on her feet. Brioni suits were at least quadruple the price of Armani. "Did it get ripped?" she demanded.

Callum grinned down at her. "I don't care. I only care if you're all right." His voice deepened, and she was so smitten by him in this moment she could barely keep on her feet. Callum Hawk—*the* Callum Hawk—cared if she was all right?

———

Find *Her Billionaire Boss Fake Fiancé* on Amazon.

# ALSO BY CAMI CHECKETTS

**The Hidden Kingdom Romances**

*Royal Secrets*

*Royal Security*

*Royal Doctor*

*Royal Mistake*

*Royal Courage*

*Royal Pilot*

*Royal Imposter*

*Royal Baby*

*Royal Battle*

*Royal Fake Fiancé*

**Secret Valley Romance**

*Sister Pact*

*Marriage Pact*

*Christmas Pact*

**Famous Friends Romances**

*Loving the Firefighter*

*Loving the Athlete*

*Loving the Rancher*

*Loving the Coach*

*Loving the Sheriff*

*Loving the Contractor*

*Do Rely on Your Protector*

*Do Kiss the Superstar*

*Do Tease the Charming Billionaire*

*Do Claim the Tempting Athlete*

*Do Depend on Your Keeper*

**Strong Family Romance**

*Don't Date Your Brother's Best Friend*

*Her Loyal Protector*

*Don't Fall for a Fugitive*

*Her Hockey Superstar Fake Fiance*

*Don't Ditch a Detective*

*Don't Miss the Moment*

*Don't Love an Army Ranger*

*Don't Chase a Player*

*Don't Abandon the Superstar*

**Steele Family Romance**

*Her Dream Date Boss*

*The Stranded Patriot*

*The Committed Warrior*

*Extreme Devotion*

**Quinn Family Romance**

*The Devoted Groom*

*The Conflicted Warrior*

*The Gentle Patriot*

*The Tough Warrior*

*Her Too-Perfect Boss*

*Her Forbidden Bodyguard*

**Running Romcom**

*Running for Love*

*Taken from Love*

*Saved by Love*

**Cami's Collections**

*Survive the Romance Collection*

*Mystical Lake Resort Romance Collection*

*Billionaire Boss Romance Collection*

*Jewel Family Collection*

*The Romance Escape Collection*

*Cami's Firefighter Collection*

*Strong Family Romance Collection*

*Steele Family Collection*

*Hawk Brothers Collection*

*Quinn Family Collection*

*Cami's Georgia Patriots Collection*

*Cami's Military Collection*

*Billionaire Beach Romance Collection*

*Billionaire Bride Pact Collection*

*Echo Ridge Romance Collection*

*Texas Titans Romance Collection*

*Snow Valley Collection*

*Christmas Romance Collection*

*The Fearless Groom*

*The Trustworthy Groom*

*The Beastly Groom*

*The Irresistible Groom*

*The Determined Groom*

*The Devoted Groom*

## Billionaire Beach Romance

*Caribbean Rescue*

*Cozumel Escape*

*Cancun Getaway*

*Trusting the Billionaire*

*How to Kiss a Billionaire*

*Onboard for Love*

*Shadows in the Curtain*

## Billionaire Bride Pact Romance

*The Resilient One*

*The Feisty One*

*The Independent One*

*The Protective One*

*The Faithful One*

*The Daring One*

## Park City Firefighter Romance

*Rescued by Love*

*Reluctant Rescue*

*Stone Cold Sparks*

*Snowed-In for Christmas*

**Echo Ridge Romance**

*Christmas Makeover*

*Last of the Gentlemen*

*My Best Man's Wedding*

*Change of Plans*

*Counterfeit Date*

**Snow Valley**

*Full Court Devotion: Christmas in Snow Valley*

*A Touch of Love: Summer in Snow Valley*

*Running from the Cowboy: Spring in Snow Valley*

*Light in Your Eyes: Winter in Snow Valley*

*Romancing the Singer: Return to Snow Valley*

*Fighting for Love: Return to Snow Valley*

**Other Books by Cami**

*Seeking Mr. Debonair: Jane Austen Pact*

*Seeking Mr. Dependable: Jane Austen Pact*

*Saving Sycamore Bay*

*Oh, Come On, Be Faithful*

*Protect This*

*Blog This*

*Redeem This*

*The Broken Path*

*Dead Running*

*Dying to Run*

*Fourth of July*

*Love & Loss*

*Love & Lies*

# ABOUT THE AUTHOR

Cami is a part-time author, part-time exercise consultant, part-time housekeeper, full-time wife, and overtime mother of four adorable boys. Sleep and relaxation are fond memories. She's never been happier.

Join Cami's VIP list to find out about special deals, giveaways and new releases and receive a free copy of *Seeking Mr. Debonair: The Jane Austen Pact* by going to this site - https://dl.bookfunnel.com/38lc5oht7r

Cami is the author of over a hundred romantic suspense novels. She is a USA Today Bestselling and award-winning author.

Hugs and happy reading!

cami@camichecketts.com
www.camichecketts.com

facebook.com/CamiCheckettsAuthor

twitter.com/camichecketts

instagram.com/camicheckettsbooks

amazon.com/Cami-Checketts/e/B002NGXNC6/ref=sxts_entity_1_bsx_s_def_r00_t_aufl?pd_rd_w=0B0n9&pf_rd_p=c227778c-e6e6-4d97-8a5a-0854898f1e10&pf_rd_r=DX4DYK796QAC0SEYF-PV4&pd_rd_r=0edd556d-1ce2-4369-81c9-c8df05bebc93&pd_rd_wg=FJEth&qid=1573271538

bookbub.com/profile/cami-checketts

# ROYAL SECRETS - EXCERPT

Julia Adams stepped out into the lamplit street in front of the quaint cottage she was staying in and started into a jog. She could hear the waves past the thick hedge on her right. Hopefully she could pop through the tropical wall and out onto the beach soon. It was four a.m. and still pitch-black outside, but her internal clock was all messed up. She had spent over twenty-four hours in airplanes or airports, the last four in a puddle jumper with only her and the pilot, a handsome man named Treck who had an easy smile.

After an effective argument on her part, he'd confessed his connections to the hidden island of Magna's royal family. The confession had made Julia even more excited to meet the elusive and supposedly beautiful people. Treck kept her entertained with stories of his and the second royal son's exploits. It sounded like Prince Bodi Magnum had quite the inventive mind. At least the stories had kept her distracted as they flew over teal-colored ocean and she prayed the rattling, bouncing airplane would make it.

She'd landed after dark. A beautiful young lady, Zara Lancelot —apparently the royal family's assistant—had been waiting for her. She had taken Julia straight to the cottage that was only a few minutes from the castle and the other royal residences. Julia had seen the towering castle lights, the steeples of a church, and some town lights, but it had been too late for a tour. She couldn't wait to witness the exquisite kingdom with her own eyes.

Prince Bodi Magnum had contacted her brother's marketing agency and asked for a top executive to help him create and market trips to the island of Magna, known to the world as the Hidden Kingdom because of how private and secluded it was. The prince already had ideas such as a medieval jousting tournament and fair, beach and mountain exploration, and the charm of an entire country set in the past. Julia had begged until Justin had finally acquiesced and given her the job.

Now she was here and ready to explore despite the early hour. A run on the beach and a long shower and she'd be ready to evaluate and advise Prince Bodi. It was so magical here. She'd caught glimpses of the towering, well-lit castle and the old-fashioned lamps lighting the streets as the rickety plane had landed. Those same lamps now lit her way, but she really wanted to be on that beach. She could hear the waves rolling in now. Any minute now, she'd find an opening in the hedge. Would the sand be soft or hard-packed? A few pictures she'd found online that had leaked from the island showed lush mountain ranges, a gorgeous royal city, and farms and ranches scattered over the rest of the island.

Julia increased her pace as the pounding of the waves on the sand grew louder and her excitement mounted. She finally found a break in the hedgerow and darted through it onto the dark beach. She was blinded for a second by the lack of lamplight on this side of the hedge. She ran smack into a wall—a moving wall.

A wall of flesh and muscle.

"Oomph," she gasped as she rebounded toward the ground.

A hard body fell with her onto the sand. Warm, strong arms wrapped around her as the person rolled quickly and took the brunt of the impact. It was a matter of seconds before they settled in the sand. Julia was stunned, but she dimly realized she was cocooned in a man's arms. Her heart raced and her stomach gave a little lurch. Something about this man holding her was both stimulating and comforting.

"Are you all right?" a cultured, smooth voice asked.

"Um ... I think so. Did I take you out?"

The man chuckled easily. Julia's eyes adjusted to the dim moonlight and she was gifted with the sight of a handsome face, all manly lines, with thick dark brows and penetrating dark eyes. "I think I may have taken you out. I saw a shadow dart out of the hedge, but I reacted too slowly. Forgive me."

"Sure." Julia tried to move, but he held her so tightly that she couldn't squirm free. Part of her didn't want to be free, but she didn't know this man and she shouldn't want to languish in his arms. "Um ... excuse me."

"Oh! Forgive me again." He released his hold on her and jumped to his feet, bending to help her up. His hands remained on her elbows, tracing warmth through her flesh. He stared at her. "You're an outsider?"

She backed up a step and his hands fell away. Losing his warm touch was regrettable, but she wondered about his tone. Did he not like outsiders? Was he going to take her up to the volcano and sacrifice her for not fitting in? Nobody knew much about Magna, but it was rumored that the Hidden Kingdom had some archaic traditions. She'd heard that the island's inhabitants were graced with olive skin and dark hair and eyes. Her red hair and blue eyes would definitely stand out.

"How'd you guess?" She forced a bright tone and prayed he wasn't the druid guardian of the beach, intent on keeping outsiders from invading his peaceful island.

She needed to stop reading fantasy books.

A smile crinkled his cheeks, creating nice laugh lines around his eyes and mouth. "I've never seen a redhead anywhere but on the television screen."

"Sheltered life, eh?" She tossed her long red ponytail. As a child, she'd hated the attention she received because of her coloring, but she didn't mind it now. It helped that her hair had darkened to a deep reddish brown over the years. "What do you think?"

His eyes trailed over her and warmed her all the way through. "It's beautiful," he murmured. "May I?"

"May you what?"

"Touch your hair."

She blinked at him. "I don't think we're that friendly," she said, though a large part of her longed to give him permission to touch her hair, her hand, or maybe wrap her up in his arms again. Her eyes had fully adjusted now, and she liked the lean lines of his arms revealed in his short-sleeved shirt.

He chuckled and said, "Forgive me. What brings you to Magna, Miss Red?"

She arched an eyebrow. Something in his eyes said he knew

exactly who she was and why she was here, but he obviously wanted to tease her. "You've never met an outsider before, eh?"

"Not one as beautiful as you."

She wanted to accept his compliment, but his nickname from before still stung. "Well, here's a tip. Us outsiders don't like being made fun of for the color of our hair."

He gave her an alluring smirk that made her lean closer without intending to. "Even though we are 'not that friendly,' I should explain that I wasn't making fun of you but giving a compliment. You are undoubtedly the most beautiful and exotic woman I've ever seen."

Her dark-red hair garnered attention in America, but nobody had ever said she was "beautiful and exotic." She wanted to giggle like a teenager, but instead she said, "Nope, sorry. We are not friendly enough for you to give me an empty compliment." She flipped her hair over her shoulder and jogged around him and along the sandy beach. It was soft sand and slow going.

He caught up with her easily. "I hope I have the chance to become 'friendly' with you on your visit to our beautiful island." She couldn't place his smooth accent, probably because she'd never heard it before, but she loved the way he talked.

"Is this your personal island?" she asked, trying to discern his expression in the dim light, but it was harder now that they were moving.

He smiled, but his answer gave nothing away. "All Magnites feel this is their personal island. We're very proud of our beautiful country and our heritage."

"I see. And what are you doing jogging so early in the morning?"

"Patrolling for redheaded intruders."

She stared at him, hit a rock with her foot, and would have gone down if he hadn't reached out to steady her. His touch brought fire to her arm and she wasn't sure she was ready to be attracted to some local who was either teasing her or was a military sentinel of some sort. Gently tugging her arm free, she walked instead of trying to run in the thick sand. He slowed to keep pace with her.

"You're teasing me," she decided. "You don't actually patrol for intruders."

"I am teasing you," he admitted. "We have military boats who patrol for intruders. The closest island is a hundred and eighty two miles away, so it's rare we get curious teenagers coming by."

"Why are Magnites so private?" she asked. Some lights appeared to their left on the beach, another small cottage with warm light spilling from the windows.

"Magna used to be one of the wealthiest nations in the world because of the gold mined for hundreds of years from our mountains. In years past, we had to fight hard to protect our wealth and our people's independence and privacy. The gold has been gone for over twenty years now. We are still a fiercely proud people, but we lack the currency or military power to back it up. We have very little to trade because of our isolation and lack of shipping ability, but we are mostly self-sufficient due to our mild climate and hard-working people."

"That might be why I'm here," she mused. She'd had no idea Magna might be in financial trouble. "Prince Bodi asked me to come ..." Her voice trailed off as he glanced sharply at her and she realized the prince might not appreciate her spilling her purpose or ideas to some handsome guy on the beach.

"Prince Bodi asked you to come?" he prompted.

"I'm sorry. I don't know if I'm at liberty to say."

He gave her a slight smile. "We are 'not that friendly,' eh?"

She laughed, grateful he seemed so easy going. She probably should've been more leery on the beach alone in the pre-dawn hours, but this well-built man seemed protective, intriguing, and well-mannered. "No, we are not." They walked in silence for a few steps, and she saw some faint pinpricks of light up on a mountain peak. She couldn't wait for the sun to rise. Maybe she could get a tour of the island before her real work began. "Do you know Prince Bodi?"

"Very well." His voice was confident; he didn't seem intimidated by the prince at all. Was he military, truly patrolling for intruders? Maybe he reported straight to the prince and would inform him that his new marketing associate was loose-lipped.

"What's he like?" Treck had given her all kinds of stories and insight, but he was the prince's closest friend, in his words, so his opinion might be skewed. She'd like to hear from another local what the second royal son was like.

"He's incredible—kind, hard-working, smart, charming, handsome." He glanced askance at her, his eyes dancing with humor.

"Are you sure you didn't just describe yourself?" she deadpanned.

He roared at that. "I suppose all those characteristics could apply to me as well." He sobered. "Truthfully, Bodi's a good man and a good friend. I think you'll enjoy working with him on ... whatever you're doing."

"Thank you. I'd better ... get my run in and get ready for the day."

"Is this where you're intoning I should run back the other direction?"

She didn't want him to, but it wasn't smart to encourage him. He was attractive and appealing, but she wasn't here to meet a man. She was here to work, and maybe help this country more than she'd imagined. She loved the idea of rescuing them from financial doom. Julia Adams riding up on her white steed, saving the kingdom and the handsome prince. She smiled to herself. Just being on this incredible island made her imagine she was in a fairy tale.

"Does that smile mean you don't want me to run away?"

"I like to run alone," she insisted, though truthfully she would like more time with this handsome, intriguing man. The island was small enough that she was sure to see him again.

"I know when it's time to make an exit." He saluted her and turned the other direction. "Goodbye, Miss Red. It was a pleasure meeting your beautiful self this beautiful morning."

She turned and faced him instead of jogging away as she should. "The pleasure was all mine, oh druid guardian of the beach—or what should I call you?"

"Druid guardian of the beach is fine, but my friends call me PB."

"Peanut butter?"

He chuckled. "Yes, ma'am. Do you like peanut butter?"

"It depends if it's creamy or chunky."

His smile deepened those laugh lines that she liked. "Definitely creamy. I'm smooth and charming and *definitely* creamy."

Her stomach somersaulted again. She wished the sun was up so she could see exactly how deep brown those eyes were. "Too bad. I prefer chunky."

She whirled and ran off down the beach as his laughter floated in the air behind her. She smiled to herself. She wouldn't soon forget their conversation; what a warm and intriguing welcome to the country of Magna. She hoped she'd see PB again.

———

Find *Royal Secrets* on Amazon.